RHYS

The K9 Files, Book 17

Dale Mayer

RHYS: THE K9 FILES, BOOK 17
Beverly Dale Mayer
Valley Publishing Ltd.

ISBN-13: 978-1-773365-54-1
Print Edition

Books in This Series

About This Book

Welcome to the all new K9 Files series reconnecting readers with the unforgettable men from SEALs of Steel in a new series of action packed, page turning romantic suspense that fans have come to expect from USA TODAY Bestselling author Dale Mayer. Pssst… you'll meet other favorite characters from SEALs of Honor and Heroes for Hire too!

Rhys hadn't expected a trip to Cottage Grove, Oregon to start with a house being shot up with bullets. If it had stopped there it would have been manageable. A drive by shooting that the cops should be able to chase down. But nothing was easy in his world. And this case went to hell right from the beginning…

Taylor, an army vet herself was struggling to regain a normal life after she was injured by friendly fire in Iraq. Taking on a war dog appealed as it gave her a connection that they could both relate too, but she had to pass some kind of interview before she could keep Tallahassee. An interview with someone with a prosthetic just like hers. Only he was far more capable than she was.

Still that was the least of her worries as things go from bad to worse and she realizes these attacks were very personal… and very close to home…

Sign up to be notified of all Dale's releases here!
https://geni.us/DaleNews

PROLOGUE

B ADGER LOOKED OVER at Kat, as they sat in their living room, and asked, "How did you get to be so smart?"

"I didn't get to be smart at all," she said. "I just knew something was there about his ex-wife, but I had no idea that he just needed to make peace with her. I figured he needed to deal with something."

"Well, not only did he make peace with her—in the sense that they have spoken and have agreed to ignore each other—but her much-older husband is also not so happy to have her younger ex-husband in town. So Silas is chomping at the bit over that." Badger laughed. "Not to mention the squatter seemed to do this elsewhere. Jenner did the sheriff's job and checked in nearby counties, so that guy is sitting in jail, and the sheriff's not happy to be shown up by Jenner either. But better than that, Jim is home, and Jenner will stay in town to help him fix up the place for wheelchair access."

"I think that's a great idea." Kat looked over at Badger. "Is there any spare money to help out with some supplies?" Badger rolled his eyes at her. She grinned and added, "Well, I'll help out with the prosthetic. I just figured that maybe they needed some building supplies to handle the modifications."

"Absolutely they do," Badger agreed. "I'll talk to the guys about it."

She nodded. "You do that."

Such a note of satisfaction filled her voice that he grinned at her. "You, my dear, are one very manipulative prosthetic genius."

"Only when it counts." She walked over and sat down on his lap, wrapped her arms around him, and said, "Besides, it's a happy story all around. How can we not like that?"

"It's perfect. Jim'll keep both dogs at his revamped childhood home, and even Kellie is getting comfortable being around them. I don't see Jenner being dogless for long."

"No, and I think it's a great idea that Jenner sets up a way to help veterans. I mean, it'll take some time to coordinate, but he'll be somebody else for us to send people to."

"Ah." Badger laughed. "You've got a soft heart, my dear."

"I do, but the good thing is, it belongs to you." She wrapped her arms tighter around him and kissed him. Then she twisted in his arms and asked, "What's this?" She pointed to the end table beside them.

"The next file."

"Wow. Have you got somebody for it?"

"Nope, not yet. Jager thought he might know somebody. One of his neighbors. I guess their son came home, looking a little worse for wear."

"Right. It's hard to imagine how many out there aren't even on our radar."

"Well, this guy came back from a mission over in Iraq, got blown up—a story we all know—and maybe he needs to talk to you. I'm not so sure yet, but apparently a dog over there died in the same accident and he's really heartsick over it. They were moving the forward operating base, when they got blown up. So he's looking to find something else in his life to find meaning."

"Oh, I like this already. Where will we send him?"

"*We?*" he asked, raising his eyebrows.

"Absolutely. This is a *we* job."

He smiled and agreed. "It is, indeed."

"And where's the dog?"

"In Oregon."

She frowned at that.

"Why, what's wrong with Oregon?" he asked her.

"Oregon's fine, but I hope it's an okay scenario for our War Dog and our next man."

"This *is* a different scenario. We haven't had one of these before."

"And what does that mean?"

"Apparently a woman picked up the dog, contacted the ASPCA, found it was tagged, came up as one of the War Dogs, and they want somebody to go check on it."

"She wants to keep it? Because, if that's the case, it would be a good thing. Right?"

"She does want to keep the dog but is concerned about its training. She hasn't had much."

"What about this guy you are sending? Has he any experience with K9s?"

"Well, he was a trainer, so, in a way, it's a match made in heaven."

She looked up at him, and a glint came into her eyes.

He nodded. "I knew you wouldn't miss that reference. Apparently she's also ex-military, and she's got her own prosthetic. Although she's struggling with it and was hoping this dog would be more of a therapy animal."

Kat's frown flashed again. "I don't know that the War

Dogs have that kind of temperament."

"I don't think she's looking to get it registered, just more of a case of she's alone and could use it for mental health purposes, like an emotional support dog."

"In that case, you're right. It sounds like a match made in heaven."

"I hope so, but I've got to get a hold of this guy first."

Just then came a knock on the open door, and Jager walked in and pointed. "This is actually him. *Rhys.*"

The man leaned against the doorframe, his arms crossed over his chest.

"The one I was telling you about."

"Right." Badger nodded. He looked over at Kat and then at the closed file. He asked his wife, "What do you think?"

She studied Rhys and decided immediately. "Let's do it."

CHAPTER 1

R HYS GORMAN STEPPED from his truck, parked beside
the gas pump, and waited for the attendant. He was
here, wherever *here* was. He turned and looked around,
studying the area. It was a quaint, very picturesque town, but
not a place he'd ever been before.

Cottage Grove, Oregon, is what the sign stated. He'd
seen elsewhere that this area was often compared to Parke
County, Indiana, the Covered Bridge Capital of the US,
which was something else he'd never really seen before. He
wondered if it really was the stated capital of the US or just
more about the western coast.

Often people made the mistake—wherever they lived—
that the whole world revolved around them. Rhys almost
smiled at that but was then reminded of his very smothering
scenario back at home, so he had taken this chance to come
here, confronting his fear of losing another dog.

Kat had been very persuasive, and she would help him
get a prosthetic that fit and worked for him, which was huge.
In the meantime he was stuck with his old one, while his leg
healed and while she took measurements and worked on a
prototype. She'd certainly seemed positive about it, and he
hadn't even realized this was the work that she did, until he'd
looked her up after talking to his friend Jager. He'd known
Jager for a while, and, if it weren't for him, Rhys probably

wouldn't have stepped inside Kat's office at all.

And maybe it would have been better if he hadn't. Hell, maybe this whole thing would have been better if he'd just walked away and told Badger and Kat to find somebody else for this op. The last thing Rhys wanted to do was get emotionally involved with a dog. He could handle all kinds of stress and trauma, and yet, the minute a dog was involved, he went to pieces. And it was stupid. He'd been bugged about it plenty.

However, he'd also like to think that he hadn't lost his humanity in all those years that he'd been in the navy. After a stint in the military, it was hard sometimes to remember that some humanity remained in the world. He'd gotten jaded and old and tired of dealing with the problems that he'd faced over and over again.

His injury had just about finished him. He wasn't alone in that thinking; several others of his unit had gone down at the same time. They were all still trying to pick up the pieces of their world and to make something out of it. Something different than the rest. And, for that reason alone, Rhys rarely spoke about it and had pushed away his parents from even asking any questions because he didn't want to be rude and tell them to stuff it. But he'd made it very clear to his father that Rhys would give no answer, so to stop asking, before he left town and before he chose to have nothing to do with them.

His father didn't like his answer, but he'd given Rhys a single nod. "Fine. We weren't happy when you went into the navy, and, you coming home in this shape, obviously we're even unhappier," he explained, "but this is your choice."

"It is," Rhys muttered. "It is my choice, and it's the only thing I have left to live by, so honor it, or I'm out of here."

His father had immediately agreed, and Rhys hadn't been there for his father's conversation with his mom, but Rhys was pretty sure that it was rough on both of them. Yet that's just the way it needed to be if they kept hounding him because he just couldn't handle speaking about his accident and the immediate fallout he had endured. It shouldn't even have come to that. This break from his family would be good.

Rhys didn't know if he would go back or not; going home after coming out of the hospital had been tough enough. He'd been there for three months in a room over the garage, while he sorted out his life and tried to get through the additional therapy he needed. The fact that he'd even had to go home had hurt. It wasn't something anybody should have to do, particularly not in the shape that he was in. But it's the only option he had left, so, whatever.

At the time he'd thought maybe it'd be nice to go home. However, his mother couldn't stop the nagging, combined with the guilt trips, atop the constant pushing to eat—as if food solved every problem in the world. Then she resorted to the smothering repetitive questions, like, "Are you okay?" *Hell no, I'm not okay. I'm far from okay.*

So going home had stopped Rhys's hopes that the situation would be nice, and it had turned into being emotionally painful. Rhys shouldn't have gone home. It had been too much for his mom. She'd been heartbroken to see him, and that had just made it way worse, made him feel like he was some sort of a freak. Even though his father had tried hard to calm her down, she wasn't the kind to calm down. She was all about hysteria. Whereas his dad was stoic.

And right now? The last thing Rhys needed was anybody making a caterwauling mess of his world.

He was also a private person, even more so since his surgeries.

Shaking that off, he thanked the gas attendant, walked inside and paid with his credit card, grabbed his receipt and got back into his truck. He punched in the address to double-check his directions and then pulled out onto the road. Taylor wasn't far away, which was a good thing. He'd help her and Tallahassee, starting today. At the same time Rhys figured that a couple days might be enough to get him out of his emotional hell, long enough that he could get a break and could figure out what he would do with his life. And it seemed foolish at this age, at this stage, to even have to consider these things. But it was what it was.

Wondering at the fool's errand he was on, Rhys headed down several small country roads, past a quaint little town center, and headed on through to the other side. When he got to the address, it was a small house, at least from the first pass he made, with a sidewalk leading to a picturesque front entrance and a long veranda, beautiful gardenias climbing up the side of the house. It was a large property, something he could really appreciate. He stared at it.

It seemed almost fairy tale-ish.

Something that he no longer believed in. Something that he didn't think anybody should believe in, ever. The reality was what he experienced out in the world, and it was a bitch to come back from that. He didn't want to park on her driveway just yet, not sure of his welcome. So he parked on the opposite shoulder of the road, turned off the engine, and, just as he went to open the driver's side door, another truck drove by him very slowly and then slowed down more when it got to her place. The driver had a baseball cap pulled down low, and, even as Rhys watched, the driver lifted a handgun, pointed it through the passenger window and started firing at the woman's house, before the gunman hit the gas and ripped off into the distance.

Rhys didn't give it a second thought; he immediately turned his vehicle around and chased after the gunman.

TAYLOR MOORE HUDDLED in a corner of the dining room, between the kitchen and the living room, her arms wrapped around her chest, rocking in place, shuddering. The damn bullets. She didn't even know if they were hitting the house, hitting her, hitting her car, hitting anything—even if they were bullets—but it just took her right back to the damn event that sent her tumbling and spiraling out of control, landing in the world that she currently lived in.

She didn't even know what would set it off; sometimes it was just a vehicle backfiring, and, if that's all it was, she almost hated herself for her constant overreaction. She understood the PTSD part of it; she understood that she would have to learn to deal with the trauma. She understood all that. But what she didn't understand was how she was supposed to do any of it when she was constantly crippled by some of the simplest noises.

So much anger was inside her, so much that she couldn't reconcile, so much that she couldn't find peace with, and, of course, that's what her psychologist wanted her to confront. Yet they didn't give her the tools to do it. They gave her all this mumbo-jumbo about working on the problems. They wanted her to take drugs, so it would become something that was much easier to deal with.

She didn't want to take drugs. She just wanted to find a

way through this nightmarish maze to a world where she could function properly. She slowly lifted her head, hearing a harsh whine at the door and claws jumping up, trying to get in. She got up slowly, using the wall for support, and hobbled her way over, where she opened the door and looked out. There was her dog, outside the screen, whining at her, his tail going crazy. She opened the screen and reached out a hand. Immediately his soft nose shoved into it. "I'm fine," she told him.

But he apparently didn't believe her and kept nudging and nudging at her.

Finally she opened the door wider and murmured, "This isn't a good idea."

But she seemed helpless to stop it, as the dog raced inside. However, instead of coming to her for more cuddles, he took off and did a full search of the house. She leaned against the door, watching him. "I don't know what it was," she admitted. "Believe me. I don't really want to do a postmortem on this either."

But again he just ignored her, on his own path of some thought processes that she couldn't seem to access. She wondered what he heard when she heard the same sounds. What the hell was going on that she was such a mess? She slowly walked over to the kitchen and put on the teakettle. After an episode like that, which just seemed to take apart everything in her world, she was always exhausted. Yet here she was, safe in her own home, and still didn't have that sense of security that she was desperate for.

As the dog raced back into the kitchen, his nose still to the ground, she asked, only half joking, "What are you, part bloodhound?"

But his ears were calm, and his tail was wagging, as he

stepped closer and gave her a *woof* and then shoved his big nose into her hand once more. She would have crouched down but her ankle joint didn't work so well. She bent over instead and gave him a good cuddle. "I don't know what that was which you just did, but thanks for keeping an eye out," she muttered.

Of course, keeping an eye out was a whole different thing when you were a dog, but, hey, she'd take the fact that anybody cared, even a canine. With a hot cup of tea now in her hand, she put a leash on the dog and slowly made her way back out to the front of the house, where she sat down on the porch and stared. She didn't even know why she was out here. Except maybe confronting the terror for her to be out here. She refused to let that become her world too. Seemed like everything had narrowed down to what she could handle and what she couldn't, and 99 percent of it fell into that *what she couldn't handle* department.

And it sucked. In a big way. She used to be sociable. Until everything in the military had blown up. She used to have friends, until they took one look at her now and saw the shape she was in, and they made polite excuses and ran.

She could hardly blame them. She wasn't exactly anything to look at anymore, and she sure as hell wasn't anything nice to be around. Not that it was her fault. It was nobody's fault, including theirs. It's just the way of it. And she was working at finding acceptance, but, in her heart of hearts, she knew that would take a lot longer.

This isn't who she wanted to be. She wanted to be the person she had left behind, when she went into the military, the one full of hope, the one full of patriotism, the one who was doing this because it was the right thing to do. Not this broken-down beat-up person who, so embittered even before her accident, that even now she found it hard to find any way forward. She knew who was responsible for a lot of that pre-accident part of her army life, and none of it made any difference because *he* wouldn't pay the price. She was the one paying the price.

And would continue to pay the price for a long time yet.

She wanted to be healthy and whole; she wanted to see her way through all this, and yet all she saw was more nightmares, more pain, more intolerances that she struggled with, and how the hell was she supposed to find anything that made her happy about that? If only there was another answer, if only … she hadn't gone to the military police to turn him in.

Was it his fault where she was at now? Not likely. But he was ultimately the start of all this. And that was something that she found almost impossible to deal with. As she sat here on the porch, a truck pulled up to the front of the house. Immediately the dog stood up and studied the approaching vehicle. When it parked, and the engine turned off, she wondered idly which neighbor was visiting her.

When the man stepped out, making absolutely no attempt to hide the prosthetic on his leg, she stared. And then her heart sank.

"Better not be coming here," she muttered to herself.

Almost immediately the dog beside her growled.

She looked over at him. "Is that because of me or because of him?" she muttered to the dog.

The dog didn't say anything but watched with a hawk's eyes. As the man approached the small gate and unlocked it, stepping forward, he looked around carefully, catching sight of her. And then, with a nod, he called out, "Good afternoon."

She shook her head. "There's nothing good about it. I don't know what you're doing here or what business you think you have, but you're not welcome."

He stopped, stared, and then nodded. "And maybe that dog beside you has a different greeting for me."

And, sure enough, she looked down to see the dog, his tail going like crazy, a whine starting to come out of the back of his throat.

The stranger entered the gate and slowly approached. "I mean you no harm."

She looked from him to the dog, who was straining at his leash. Immediately the man held up his hand in some sort of a command, and the dog's butt hit the porch floor, but it couldn't stop wiggling with joy. And, with that reaction, she unhooked the leash. "Well, isn't that just something?" Her heart sank, as she realized that this man had a claim to this dog that she could never hope to have.

The dog barreled toward him, jumping up on him, knocking him backward against the fence. Instead of being upset, the man just laughed, wrapped his arms around the dog, and held him close. At least as close as anybody could during such a wiggling embrace. When the dog finally got free again, he jumped down, doing zoomies all over the front yard.

She'd never seen him act like this before. Didn't think it would ever happen again. It was such normal dog behavior that she was happy for him, but, at the same time, she was sad because she hadn't given him that sense of confidence, that sense of freedom, to be who he needed to be. And yet here this stranger walked up, opened the gate, and there he was, giving her dog what he needed.

He looked at her slowly, took a couple steps forward,

and asked, "May I come up?"

She stared at him resentfully and then shrugged. "You're already in, so you might as well."

He nodded and walked a few steps closer. "Thank you."

"What for?" she asked suspiciously.

"For looking after Tallahassee here," he replied.

"He's your dog?" she asked.

Immediately he looked at her and shook his head. "No, but he was part of … a training unit that I worked with when I was in the navy."

"Navy?" She frowned.

"I was part of a special unit that worked with dogs," he added. "Tallahassee was one of them."

"And how do you know his name? I've been calling him Fred."

"Fred?" He shook his head, whistled, and called out, "Tallahassee, come."

The dog immediately raced over and jumped up again.

At Rhys's command, Tallahassee stopped jumping. Rhys turned toward her. "His name's Tallahassee," he repeated. "As you can see, he responds to it quite well."

"Did you know he was here? Is that why you've come?" she asked suspiciously.

He immediately took a slow step back, as if realizing something in her world was flipping, and he understood that he was causing it.

She shook her head at the stranger's retreat and his lack of an answer. "Why are you here?" she repeated, her heart in her throat at the thought of losing the dog. She could only take so many losses in life—although she'd been prepared to lose this dog if it didn't work out for her, which was selfish on her part. She hadn't in any way expected somebody else to show up with a prior claim. But, after what she'd seen, it was obvious this man definitely had a prior claim.

The man looked at her gently and said, "Before we discuss any of that, can you tell me if you're okay?"

She looked at him. "I don't know what you mean."

"What I mean," he stated, "is about whoever shot into your house. Did they hit anything? Are you hurt?"

She stared at him. "Shot?" Her voice was faint, her heart slamming against her chest.

The stranger's eyes narrowed, and he nodded slowly. "You didn't hear it?"

"I, … I did," she confirmed, reaching a hand to her temple. She closed her eyes. "I just wasn't sure if it was real or not."

"You didn't imagine it," he declared, his voice harsh. "Somebody drove by and shot into your house multiple times."

CHAPTER 2

TAYLOR DIDN'T EVEN know what to say. Finally she gasped out, "Shots?"

He nodded. "He lifted a handgun, while I was parked across the street, and fired into the house. I'm not sure what he was firing or what his intentions were," he noted calmly, studying her with a gaze that she found intensely unnerving. "But obviously something's going on."

"Maybe it was random," she murmured. She felt that jump of hope at such a suggestion, but, even as soon as she mentioned it, she knew it was wrong. She gave a hard swallow and got up and bolted inside the house. He followed but stayed close to the front door. She stood in the living room. clenching her hands together.

"Do you want to tell me what kind of trouble you're in?"

She immediately spun and looked at him. "Why are you here?" she asked bluntly.

He hesitated, then shrugged. "I came to check on Tallahassee," he said.

Her gaze widened. "You came to check on the dog?"

He nodded. "It may sound ridiculous to you, but we do take these War Dogs seriously. They've given a lot of their lives to save others in military service," he explained. "When the animals retire, we try hard to keep track of them and to ensure that they're getting a decent home. This one slipped through the cracks, and somehow ended up in a situation where he came to you."

She nodded. "Yes, at the shelter. I know somebody there, and they thought maybe I would be a good fit for the dog."

"And are you?" he asked bluntly.

She stared at him. "A good fit for the dog's one thing. However, like what I just saw, like how he was with you? That's something I've never seen from Fred—Tallahassee—before," she admitted. "So, if you are looking for those circumstances, then I can't say that I am. Would I love to? Yes. Would I like to get more training? Yes. I did ask for that."

"And we did hear that," he confirmed. "But these dogs, although they're not hard to look after, they do have some special needs. I looked up Tallahassee's file, and, of course, he's been through an awful lot of action. Has it bothered him?"

She stared at him. "Bothered him in what way?" she asked, her voice faint.

He shrugged. "What was he doing when the bullets hit the house?"

She shook her head. "I heard the bangs, but I didn't hear anything hitting the house."

His gaze narrowed. "I'll be back." And, with that, he stepped out the front door.

She sagged to the couch, wondering what had just happened to her world. It was bad enough what she thought she was going through. But to know that somebody had deliberately fired upon her house? That was beyond cruel. And that brought her thoughts all the way back around to who she knew most likely was behind it. And how much was that asshole behind it anyway?

Her mind couldn't even grasp how this was happening. And she needed to get it together before she looked like somebody who had completely lost it and who couldn't keep a dog. She stared down at Tallahassee, who, instead of following the stranger outside, had stayed beside her. She reached out a hand, and he came over and gently pressed his muzzle against her hand. When she looked up, the stranger was watching them interact.

He gave a nod. "Tallahassee cares."

"Maybe," she agreed, her voice faint, "but that doesn't mean it's a good fit."

"Maybe not," he noted. "Most of that'll depend on you."

She didn't know what to say. "What's your name?" she asked. "I can't believe I let you in here without even knowing who you are."

He stepped forward, pulling a card from his wallet. "This is me," he said.

"Rhys Gorman," she read aloud. "You're a trainer?"

"I am. I was," he corrected. "I vowed to never do it again because, after losing as many dogs as I have in war, I found it very difficult to handle, to process. When I saw my last action, I lost my dog at the time. I swore I'd never get back into working with animals again because the pain of losing them is so horrific. Believe me. I took a lot of ribbing for that attitude too."

She stared at him. "Why?"

"Because a lot of people don't look at animals as having the same relationship to people. Some of the guys knew exactly how I felt, but others? Not so much."

She nodded as she stared down, her hand absentmindedly stroking Tallahassee's coat. "He's a beautiful animal," she whispered.

"He is, indeed, and he certainly has taken to you," he stated.

"No, I don't think so. I think he's just—" Then she stopped, shrugged, and added, "I don't know. I don't know what he is."

"Obviously something is going on in your world. I would like to help."

She stared at him in shock. "You don't even know what it is, and you don't know who I am," she murmured. "So even saying something like that is foolish."

He stared at her with that unrelenting, unwavering gaze, and she felt herself trying to pull in and away. Yet everything inside her felt exposed, as if he could see something that she didn't want him to.

"You want to tell me what's going on?"

She immediately shook her head. "No, I don't," she replied in an attempt at bravado that she didn't feel. "You need to decide if the dog stays with me or not." When he remained silent, she added, "I need to go lie down, and, therefore, I'll shut the front door and lock it and head upstairs. And you don't get to stay." She faced him down with a look that she had perfected for a very long time, but she also knew would have absolutely no effect on him.

"That's fine," he agreed. "And, no, I'm not making that decision regarding Tallahassee right now."

"And can you make that decision?" she asked. "Is that something within the power that you have?"

"I don't know. Don't give me a reason to find out."

No threat was in those words, but she felt a chill creep over her shoulders anyway. She walked to the front door and pulled it open. "If you need any more questions answered, it'll have to happen later."

"And what good will later do?"

"I won't be quite so exhausted," she replied, "at least I hope not."

He nodded. "And how much is that exhaustion from what just happened?"

She stiffened. "I don't know what you're talking about."

"Don't lie to me," he said impatiently. "I get that something's wrong in your world right now. But you didn't call for the police, you didn't do anything, outside of sit here almost frozen, when I told you that somebody had deliberately done a drive-by shooting."

"You don't know what I might have done," she argued, "or what I might be planning to do."

"Well, the timing has already gone for calling the cops," he stated bluntly.

She looked at him. "Did you call?"

He shook his head. "No, I didn't. I wanted to talk to you first."

"Well, now you have," she murmured, as she motioned at the door. "Please leave."

He took several steps toward the door, obviously not happy about it. When Tallahassee started to bark, he stopped, looked at him, and asked, "What's up, boy?"

Tallahassee raced past the front door, now open, where they both stood.

Rhys immediately followed the War Dog, and there, in the distance, was the same damn truck, ripping down the road.

"That was him," he told her, as she came up behind him. "That's the vehicle that shot at your house."

She stared in the distance. "I didn't see it at the time. Did you get enough of a look to identify it?"

"No," he admitted. "I took off after it the first time, thinking that it was probably just a random shooting. However, the fact that he came back again means it wasn't." He turned to her and said, "So screw the nap. I need you to tell me exactly what's going on."

"Or else what?" she asked.

He stared at her before replying. "I don't know who hurt you or why, or where this is all coming from, but whatever is happening right now is not something to play around with. I've seen more trouble than I would like to ever remember, but I'm not about to leave somebody who's in trouble right now."

"You mean the dog?" She tried for a sneer, yet failed. Probably because she was desperate to talk to somebody, desperate to have answers, something concrete that she could do about this nightmare her life had become.

He shook his head. "No," he corrected her gently. "You need a friend." And he gently nudged her back inside, called Tallahassee, and slammed the door shut. "And now you've got one, whether you like it or not."

RHYS STUDIED THE woman's face, seeing the exhaustion, the stress, the shakiness. "You need to go lie down," he stated bluntly. He pulled a card from his pocket, handed it to her, and said, "This is my boss. Call him, verify that I'm here, why I'm here, and then go lie down. And we'll talk as soon as you're awake again."

She just stared at him, but such a blankness filled her

gaze that he wondered if she'd been alone for a very long time or just lived constantly under extreme stress.

He gently turned her, moved her toward the stairs, and asked, "Is your bedroom upstairs?"

She nodded. "Yes, but it's a little hard to get there."

He studied her for a moment and looked down at the prosthetic foot, a very rudimentary one, and nodded. "Have you looked into getting a better prosthetic?"

"Once I heal from the last surgery."

He grimaced. "Been there, done that." In a move that surprised even himself, he bent down, scooped her into his arms, and started up the stairs, Tallahassee racing up behind him.

"Oh my God," she said, grabbing on to him. "How can you do this? You have a missing leg yourself."

"I do," he confirmed. "I'm a little farther ahead on the surgeries than you."

"Is there ever such a thing?" she asked in a broken laugh.

He winced, hearing the stress, the defeat, the knowledge that he could relate to about everything that had gone wrong and could go wrong and in her case quite possibly had gone wrong.

"Something's going on in your world," he noted, "but we can't deal with anything until you're a little bit more cognizant and aware."

"I don't sleep anyway," she replied bluntly, as he carried her up the stairs.

"Well, you will now. Right now your job is to get into your room," he stated at the top of stairs, as he slowly lowered her to her feet. "And get some sleep."

"And if I can't?" she asked. "What will you do? You can't just order me to do something and have it happen."

He gave her half a smile. "If life were that simple, I could have solved all kinds of problems in the world."

It was obvious that she wanted to smile at that, but just so much else was wrong in her world right now that he knew that she wasn't even listening to him. "It'll be fine," he stated. "First sleep."

"How can you say, *It'll be fine*?" she asked. "There hasn't been anything fine in my world in a very long time."

"And I understand that," he confirmed. "I hear the stress in your voice. I see the fatigue in your eyes, the slump of your shoulders. I am here to tell you that there is life after whatever it is that's gone wrong, and we'll help you to get there."

She stared at him. "You don't know anything about it."

Such bitterness filled her voice. He nodded. "Right. I don't know, but, after you've had a nap, you'll tell me." He nudged her toward the open bedroom door and said, "Go. Know that Tallahassee and I will be downstairs. Nobody will come up here and get you in the meantime. You're safe."

And, with that, she gave him a blank stare, as if shocked that he even understood that much.

"I've seen faces like yours before," he explained. "I've seen the stress, the shock, the pain. You are fine, right now. I'm not leaving until I know what's going on and that you will be okay."

And, with that, he turned and slowly made his way down the stairs. Tallahassee came with him. He turned to ask her if she wanted Tallahassee upstairs with her, only to find out that she'd already closed the door. With a nod, he headed downstairs. In the kitchen he put on the teakettle, not really wanting tea, but then spied a pot of coffee sitting there. He didn't care how old it was; it would be hot, considering the light was still on under it, and that would go a long way for him right now. He poured himself a cup and headed out to the living room to call his boss.

When Jager answered the phone, Rhys asked, "What the hell did you send me into?"

Jager paused for a moment. "I just got a phone call from a woman called Taylor," he replied, "presumably the one with the dog."

"Yes. What did she ask?" Rhys was incapable of keeping the curiosity out of his voice.

"If you were legit. If this newcomer who was running roughshod over her life was somebody who she could trust."

"*Roughshod*," he repeated, rolling the word around in his mouth. "Yeah, that's probably about right."

At that, Jager let out a laugh. "Seriously? Where's your usual finesse?"

"I lost it along with a leg," he stated. "And I don't know what the hell's going on here, but that woman is under a huge stress. I just ordered her up to bed to give her a chance to recoup a bit, so that, when she comes back down, then we can have a real talk."

"What do you mean?" Jager asked.

"You have no idea what's gone on. As soon as I arrived," he said, "shit hit the fan." And he quickly explained about the drive-by shooting, Tallahassee being here, and then about the truck coming back.

"Are you serious, the truck came back?"

"Yeah. It not only came back but this was obviously a targeted hit," Rhys stated. "And she doesn't want to call the cops."

"Well, that's suspicious as hell right there."

"It is, but I think the reason she doesn't want to call the

cops is something completely different."

"And what could that possibly be?"

"I'm not sure, I'm waiting for answers from her," Rhys admitted bluntly. "But I can tell you that, if you just even saw this woman, you'd have done the same thing I did."

"Ordered her to bed? Not likely," Jager teased, with a note of humor in his voice. "They tend to take that the wrong way."

As soon as Rhys rang off, he sat down, brought out a notepad, and started making notes. He should have brought his laptop in with him. It would have been easier. But this would work for the moment. He jotted down notes about the drive-by vehicle, notes about her reaction, notes about any impressions that he'd picked up—like the fact that no bullets seemed to have hit the house, so that may be a dead end. No way to stop him from writing it all down, recording this initial interview; it was almost ingrained in him.

Solving these kinds of problems was something that he had a lot of experience with. He didn't know what the hell was exactly wrong with her world, but the fact that something was so dramatically wrong scared him. She already looked like she was dealing with a lot, and, if that drive-by shooter had been intentional because she—And he stopped, looked up, then over at Tallahassee. "Does she have PTSD?" he whispered. Tallahassee's ears twitched.

If the dog could have said something, Rhys imagined he would have had a lot to say. But, at the moment, there wasn't anything the dog could really do to help Rhys figure this out. But he thought about what effect PTSD would have on somebody as the victim of a drive-by shooting like that. He needed to ask her if this was the first time something like that had happened.

And, with that, he turned the page and started a list of questions. By the time he was done and had finished the pot of coffee, he realized that she'd been sleeping for over an hour—or at least was locked up in her room, trying to figure out how to get out of just such a conversation with him.

When he heard noises in the bathroom upstairs, he knew that she was now up and moving. As she slowly made her way down the stairs, limping, taking one step at a time, he realized she really needed to get a much better prosthetic. And, with that revelation, he sent a message to Kat.

Of course I'll help. You know that we just need an awful lot of information and that she might need to come for a visit.

With that, he put away his phone and watched as she stared at him in the living room, almost wavering on her feet. He got up and helped her to the couch. "Well, you look a little bit better but still pretty out of it."

"I think I've been out of it for a long time," she replied, yawning. She stared at him. "I did phone your boss. Although I'm not sure why I bothered."

"Why is that?"

"Well, if you gave me his number to get a reference, chances are that's exactly what he would do, was give you a good reference. Which isn't helpful if I'm trying to figure out if you're trustworthy or not."

"Then trust the dog," he suggested. "Tallahassee won't lead you the wrong way."

She stared down at the dog, who, even now, was getting up from his bed to come over and to nudge her gently with his nose. "I don't know very much about dogs," she murmured. "I was just getting to the point where I thought maybe it would be good to have—" And then she stopped.

"Companionship or a guard dog?" he asked bluntly. Her gaze flew to his. "Has somebody else done this before?"

"Done what?" she asked.

"Has somebody else," he repeated, choosing his words carefully, "potentially shot into the house?"

"You mean, another drive-by shooting? I wouldn't have thought so," she replied, "but now I don't know."

He nodded. "Well, at least that's an honest answer."

"I'm not used to lying to people," she stated stiffly.

"No, maybe not. But I think it's been a long time since you've taken a serious look at what's going on and assessed the truth."

She closed her eyes and sank back. "I suppose you finished all the coffee."

"It was old," he noted.

"Yeah, it was. I forgot about it too. I made tea earlier," she explained, "forgetting that I had a pot of coffee."

"And is that a sign of stress or are you having memory problems from the injury?"

"I don't think I'm having memory problems," she shared, "but obviously I'm fairly stressed."

"How are you feeling now?" he asked, crouched down with the dog, both in front of her.

She gave him half a smile. "Better, thank you. I didn't realize I needed sleep quite so badly."

"Are you getting any sleep at night?"

She shrugged. "Not a whole lot."

"Is that why you thought Tallahassee would be a help?"

"One of the reasons," she said cautiously, looking at him.

"Good, let's hope that that part works. Now," he added, "how about I put on some fresh coffee, and then we can talk."

"Do we have to talk?" She struggled to her feet. "Besides, I'll put on the coffee."

"Only if you want to get up and move around," he noted, watching her struggle with the need for independence. And yet her very dire need in this moment was to just collapse and to do nothing for a few days. "After your accident did you have any help?"

"Nope," she said. "Matter of fact, the friends who I thought I had just left me."

"They didn't know how to handle the injury, I presume?"

"I guess." She frowned, as she looked at him. "Did that happen to you too?"

"Turns out an awful lot of things people can't handle," he shared. "My parents are a prime example."

"Don't tell me you went home to Mom," she teased, with a raised eyebrow.

"I was definitely heading there for a few weeks to reconnect, after not having seen them for quite a few years, but going home and staying with them was a mistake. Believe me. It wasn't meant to be long-term. But, as it is, my mother couldn't stop asking questions."

"Wow, they just can't let it go, can they?" she said almost bitterly. "Like we really want to rehash all that shit for their entertainment."

"I don't think it's for their entertainment as much as for their need to understand, for their need to know exactly what their child went through."

"But it doesn't help," she stated, as she poured water into the coffee maker. "And how does knowing all those ugly details help them?"

"I'm not sure it does, but I think, in their mind, they believe that maybe they can do something to help."

"Well, there isn't any help to be had," she snapped. And then she dumped in coffee, and, as she turned on the button to the coffee maker, she turned toward him. "I don't mean to snap at you."

"I know you don't," he said, with a shrug. "Believe me. I've been where you are. I'm just a little further down that road."

"Tell me. Does the road get any easier?"

"No," he said instantly. "It really doesn't."

She froze, staring at him.

"Do you want me to lie? I won't lie," he declared. "You'll lose friends. You'll lose family. You'll lose things that you thought mattered, and I'll tell you that they don't matter. Because, if those are your kinds of friends, then you need other friends. If that's the kind of family you have, you need to ditch that part of your family." He nodded. "You have a whole new set of reality to deal with, and sometimes it'll be easy, and sometimes it'll suck big-time. Anybody who tells you anything different isn't doing you a favor by lying."

She slowly released a breath. "That truth is harsh."

"It absolutely can be. Did you want me to lie? Too bad," he said bluntly. "I had people lie to me, and finding out the reality afterward wasn't any easier."

She half smiled at that. "Okay, got it. Life sucks, and then you die."

"Nope, not quite," he disagreed. "Some parts of life suck, and then you find a way to make a life after that."

"And did you?" she asked, a challenge in her voice.

"I'm here, aren't I?" he stated, looking at her. "Do I have a full-time position in this new life? No. Will I be checking up on other War Dogs, like this? Maybe, maybe not. I don't know. Could I rekindle a career in dog training? Yes. Could I do something else? Absolutely. Have I decided? No. Those are the kinds of questions that my parents can't stop asking," he muttered. "We love them, but then sometimes you have to let them go."

She smiled at that. "They don't take it well when you tell them that."

"No, they sure don't," he agreed. "Neither do they take it well when you ask them to stop with all the questions, to give you a chance to deal, to find a way to heal. Sometimes they take it even less than kindly."

She winced. "I gather yours didn't do very well with that aspect."

"Not at all," he replied. "And, even now, I probably won't go back, if Mom can't find a way to reconcile the current me with the old me."

"And that's hard too, isn't it?" she asked, looking at him. "It's gotta be hard for her."

"Of course it is, but, at some point in time, she also has to understand that I have to look after me now and that her questioning, her constant nagging and wanting to know more, isn't helping."

"No," she said, with a shudder. "God, no."

"That's the one thing that they struggle with because our silence makes them feel shut out."

"And that's not what we're trying to do."

"And it doesn't matter what we're trying to do because, in our parents' minds, what we're effectively doing is saying, *We don't care enough to tell you the details.*"

"And yet what we really are saying, I think in a lot of ways," she murmured, "is that I care so much that I don't want you to know the details."

"From our perspective, yes. From theirs, no. And it doesn't really matter because what you have to do is what you have to do for you. Their life has been upended in the sense that their child has been injured, but you're the one who has to deal with it. You're the one who has to find a new world after this," he explained. "And you have to do that in whatever way you can. And I can guarantee you that it won't be in a way that makes everybody else happy."

CHAPTER 3

T AYLOR POURED COFFEE, and then, with Rhys at her side, she awkwardly moved into the living room.

"You haven't answered me," he said a moment later.

"No," she replied. "I wasn't thinking that they were actual shootings." At an odd sound from him, she looked over at him. "I know that sounds foolish, doesn't it? But I used to react to backfiring, as I used to react to shouting. I used to react to so many noises that everybody kept telling me it was all in my head and to calm down and that nothing was happening out there. And you get to the point where you believe everybody."

"PTSD?"

"Of course," she agreed, with a wave of her hand. "Isn't that something everybody goes through?"

"No, it's not something I go through."

She stared at him in shock. "Really?"

He nodded. "Do I have nightmares? Yes. Do I envision the worst things possible that could ever happen? Yes," he explained. "But it's not necessarily PTSD where I get flashbacks or where I have to deal with loud noises."

"You're lucky," she said bluntly. "I honestly wondered if it were even possible to have a life past all this because of it."

"There is absolutely. And, yes, PTSD can be crippling. It can be insane for anybody who's trying to deal with it," he noted, "but it's not impossible. It's often brought on by trauma that's unresolved, injuries that are unresolved, friends who you lost at the same time."

She didn't say anything, wondering just how much of what he had said was real. The shrinks had never asked her about any unresolved issues, but then maybe they didn't want to know. Like so much of her world, so many people didn't want to know the truth. And yet Rhys wasn't sugarcoating anything. As she studied him, she asked, "Just your leg?"

"Leg, a couple ribs, missing a kidney, lots of scarring," he shared. "My back's the worst."

She winced at that. "Yeah, you'd think that everybody who has back injuries should be entitled to a hot tub to help take the pain down."

"Wouldn't that be nice? It's in my plans to get one, as soon as I figure out where I'll buy property."

"If you're in a position to buy property," she said, "this town's pretty decent."

"Is it though?" he asked, looking at her. "It's funny because I see somebody, like you, who's dealing with so much, and I wonder that maybe this town isn't where you need to be."

"It's home," she stated. "Although there are probably some people who wish that I would not have returned, I wouldn't want to give them the satisfaction of taking away my joy of being here on my own. I have good memories of this place."

"Memories from before?"

She nodded.

"Did any of your friends go into the military with you?"

"Several," she replied. "One didn't come home. One got

out earlier than I did; whole, happy, now sees me and basically crosses the street to get to the other side."

"Guilt maybe?"

She looked at him, frowning. "Why? He didn't do this to me."

"Survivor's guilt," he noted. "It hits a lot of people."

She thought about it, shrugged. "I've no idea then. Maybe, maybe not. It's just one of those things that I can't help him deal with because I'm too busy dealing with my own shit."

He smiled at that. "So have you had many drive-by shootings?"

"I don't have a clue," she replied. "You really stunned me with that."

"What was your reaction when it happened?"

She stared at him, a flat stare that she hoped gave away nothing of the turmoil inside her.

He waved a hand. "Look. I do get it. You don't know me, but that should make it easier to talk to me. Are you cringing in the corners? Does it make you freeze? Does it send you screaming to your room, and you slam the door and crawl into the closet? What kind of reaction do you have?"

She took a slow deep breath, realizing where he was coming from. "In this case, basically I curled up in the corner of the dining room, waiting until everything in my mind calmed down. It's not a pretty sight."

"And yet it's not that bad," he noted immediately. "Now the next question is, considering this guy came back, and I don't know if he was coming back after you or after me, as a potential witness, but could somebody have done this on purpose?"

An ugly knot formed in her stomach. "What do you mean by *on purpose?*" she asked cautiously, not wanting to even think about it.

"You heard me," he stated bluntly. "Would somebody have come to you deliberately, shot at your house once, twice, half a dozen times, I don't know, with the idea of causing you stress, sending you into a session of PTSD to help you spiral downward?"

She let out a slow deep breath. "God, to have somebody do something like that …"

"Yeah, it means an asshole of the highest order," Rhys declared, without skipping a beat. "But you're not answering my question. Is anybody out there who would do something like that to you?"

"Obviously somebody's doing it, but, as for motive, I don't know," she murmured. "As far as are there any assholes in my world, yes. Absolutely assholes are in my world, but I didn't think any lived close by."

"And where would they live if they didn't live close by?"

"They're still active military, and more's the shame for that," she noted.

"You need to explain that comment."

"No, I don't," she said, starting to get angry, realizing that she would have to discuss something that she didn't want to.

He just gave her a look.

"Stop. Jesus, I don't know how you perfected that look but …"

"Doesn't matter how," he said, "but I can't help you if I don't know everything."

"You can't help anyway," she replied, wanting to get up and run, but also knowing that getting up and running wasn't possible and, even if it were, it wouldn't do any good.

Just then, outside came a series of honks.

Rhys got to his feet and raced outside and saw the same black truck, now running up and down the street, honking. He exited the small gate and took several photos of it, but it ripped around the corner and left.

One of the neighbors came out, shaking a fist.

Rhys walked over and asked him, "Hey, do you know who that guy is?"

"I don't know, but if I ever got him alone ..." he snapped. "No-good piece of shit."

"And yet you don't know him, but you don't recognize him either?"

The man shook his head. "Nope, I sure don't. Wish I did. I've reported him to the cops twice today."

"Obviously he doesn't seem to care."

"And you haven't seen any cops show up, have you?" the neighbor noted, with an eye roll. "I'm sure by the time they do, he'll be long gone to the next town."

"You think it's just somebody out to cause trouble?"

At that, the neighbor stopped, looked at him, and asked, "What else would it be?"

Rhys didn't have an answer for him. He just smiled and nodded. "Good point." And he slowly headed back inside.

As he entered the living room, he found her curled up in a ball, rocking back and forth in fetal position in the corner. And he knew in his heart of hearts that whatever the hell was going on, this asshole was out to make her life miserable. He walked over, crouched down in front of her, and asked, "Who the hell hates you this much?"

She raised her head, looked at him, and whispered, "I don't know."

"No," he disagreed. "I don't accept that. This is personal. This is beyond mischievous," he said. "This is downright evil. Somebody is after you. I just don't know why. And you need to tell me. What has happened right now in your life or in your past that's brought this on?"

She stared at him for a second. "Somebody in the military," she whispered. "I had to report them. And ever since then my life's spiraled completely out of control."

The words just broke his heart. He opened his arms, and, with a cry, she threw herself in them, and he just closed them around her and held her tight.

TAYLOR KNEW THE questions would come, no way they couldn't. But, dear God, not yet, please not yet.

At least ten, maybe fifteen minutes—hell, it was probably three times that—later she lifted her head from his arms and murmured, "I'll grab another coffee."

"Good idea," he agreed, just as he let her go and stood up with her. They walked into the kitchen, and she poured both of them a cup.

She stepped in front of the window and stared out into the darkness outside. "I didn't realize it was this late," she murmured.

"No, I didn't either. Yet I didn't get here all that early today."

She just nodded, not knowing what else to say.

"Is he likely to come back tonight?" Rhys asked her.

"I don't know. I'm not even sure who it is."

"But you have a good idea, don't you?"

And again she nodded. "But the last I heard, he wasn't

even in town. Wasn't even thinking he'd ever come back to town," she added. "I can't imagine that he would risk this much to be here."

"You might be surprised," Rhys replied. "Particularly if he thinks that you're a problem for him."

"Oh, I'm a problem for him, but not a problem that anybody'll follow through on."

"You want to explain that?"

She shrugged. "Sexual harassment is prevalent in the military," she noted. "I tolerated it as much as I could, tried not to rock the boat, just got about doing my business. But this one guy in particular wouldn't stop, wouldn't leave me alone. He wanted sexual favors, to just leave me alone basically. And I wouldn't fall for it. I wouldn't get into the game. I reported him to my superior, and then the abuse got worse, as in much worse."

"Did he rape you?"

"No," she said, "but only because I have self-defense skills. Or I had. Do I still? I don't know." She stared at her leg. "It seems foolish to even make that an issue right now, but I think about it all the time."

"Of course you do. The minute you're attacked, you have to defend yourself, and now you're in this scenario and wondering just where your skills are at."

"I can tell you that they're nowhere good enough to be what they need to be," she stated.

"So go on. What happened after you complained?"

"I believed in the system, and I kept reporting him, thinking that they would eventually do something. They brought him in, talked to him, talked to me, and basically nothing changed, absolutely nothing happened," she declared bitterly. "One day I was out loading up a truck with supplies. We both worked in supplies, but I was in the office most of the time. So I was out loading up a truck one day, and it blew up. Just like that, out of the blue, it blew up."

"And there was no reason?"

"They did an investigation. Supposedly a gas leak or some such thing," she explained, "which makes no sense because there was no smoke. There was no fire. There was nothing. Maybe it blew up on its own, maybe not."

"But you don't believe so."

"I think he did it," she stated. "And I think he thought I would die in the process. And, when I survived, I was of course injured, struggling, and was shipped home, thankfully not quite in a box but not far off," she noted, with a certain amount of bitterness that she couldn't hold back. "And I never saw him. Then once I recovered, and I was released, it's almost like he found out that I was still alive and would be okay. But …" Then she hesitated. "I don't have any proof of this. And, if it is him, he's doing it just to make my life miserable." She looked over at Rhys. "And who would do that?"

"Somebody who would also sexually harass you and then attack you in the military," he noted. "And, if you can ever prove your case, his career is over."

She shrugged. "The higher-ups didn't seem to give a shit, and, no, it hasn't been all that long, less than a year ago since I initially reported him, but I did recently contact them," she admitted. "To see what was happening with my case."

"And that could have been the trigger that brought this on. Depending on the timing."

She thought about it and nodded. "I've been back here for two months."

"And where's he from?"

She looked over at Rhys and nodded. "Here. This is his hometown."

"Oh, *nice*. And, of course, you don't want to leave town."

"No, I don't. This is my house. It was my grandmother's house. My parents lived in it while I was young and my grandmother lived in another house. When she moved into a senior's home not far from here, I bought it from her. She's the only family who I have any contact with now. I don't want to be chased away from here too. I lost my career. I lost so much—my personal confidence, my sense of self, the ability to walk down the street without looking over my shoulder. After something like that happens to you, you just, … you fall apart, but, at the same time, you survive because surviving is mandatory. Yet here and now, I'm not sure I can survive," she muttered, as she stared around. "Maybe it would be better if I left. Maybe, maybe it would be fine."

"What would he gain by scaring you?"

She stopped, stared at him, and shrugged. "I don't know. I mean, I doubt they'll reopen the investigation. They talked to him, and he was going to improve himself, behave himself after that." She snorted. "I never did see him improve or behave himself."

"Did you guys have a history before you went in?"

"Four of us signed up together," she noted. "Like I said, one died, and one's local, and he walks away every time I see him."

"Did the four of you go into the same military unit?"

She nodded. "All army. And the other two guys are still friends, as far as I know."

"Interesting," Rhys noted. "So, even if nothing else, would this other guy do something against you?"

She considered that for a moment. "I would hope not. We were good friends in school."

"But, if he's good friends with this jerk, and somehow this asshole has got him believing that you were making it all up, do you think your *good friend* would turn around and be the one doing this?"

She frowned. "I don't know, and I really would not want to think along those lines."

"Doesn't matter if you want to or not," Rhys stated bluntly. "This is what's facing you right now. Sticking your head in the sand won't help."

She gave a broken laugh. "I'd be the last person to stick my head in the sand, but that doesn't mean that I'm necessarily willing to step up and to crucify a friend of mine."

"And yet this same friend now crosses the road when you see him."

She winced at that. "Yes. Is that because he thinks I made this other guy's life miserable? I wouldn't have thought so," she replied cautiously, "but maybe that would explain it."

"It quite likely would. What are these people's names?"

She sighed. "The guy who gave me nothing but hell in my world was Colby Henge, and my maybe-still-a-friend here in town is Andrew Pickering."

"Sounds like I need to go spend some time with Andrew."

She shook her head. "Not without me."

"You know he'll talk to me easier without you being there."

"No, he won't," she disagreed. "I've known him since we were in grade school. I wouldn't be at all surprised if I could read his face and see the lies on it."

He studied her, nodded, and said, "Then tomorrow we'll go have a talk with him."

"What good would that do?" she challenged. "Chances are he knows nothing about this."

"Maybe," he replied, "and maybe you're wrong there. Maybe he knows way too much about it."

She winced. "You really think he could be the one doing this to me?"

"Are you ready to believe that he's completely innocent and isn't doing this to you?" he asked curiously.

"I want to believe he'd have nothing to do with that," she murmured, "but I can't make that judgment either way."

"Exactly," Rhys stated, "and, if you can't, do you have any idea who even could?" He paused. "Just too much is at stake here. And not the least of which is your self-respect. You need to get your life back on track."

She gave a broken laugh. "God, you make me sound like I'm pathetic."

"Not at all," he murmured.

By the time she finally ran down with bits and pieces of information to add, her stomach started to growl. She stared down at her cell phone. "My God, how did it get to be so late?"

"It doesn't matter," he murmured. "We do need some food."

She nodded. "I get that, although I'm not sure what I'm supposed to do about it."

"You can always order in something," he suggested, "or, if you've got eggs, I can cook."

She looked at him. "You're not staying here, right?"

"I am," he stated flatly. "And don't bother telling me that you won't be relieved to know I am here."

"Relieved to have an end to this nonsense," she corrected, "but I'm not sure that you're part of that."

"No, maybe not." He got up. "Let's go check out your fridge."

She snorted. "Sure, just make yourself at home."

"I will, thanks," he replied. "Otherwise I'm ordering pizza."

"Pizza wouldn't be a bad idea," she noted cautiously. "I haven't had a whole lot to eat in quite a while, so the carbs will probably be good for me."

He immediately pulled out his phone, checking for a pizza place close by, and asked, "Which one? Belly Up? Or this Mario's Pizza?"

"Mario's Pizza," she said instantly. "Plus it's run by friends of mine."

"Place the order," he suggested, "or I will."

She waved a hand. "You can."

"Do you care what's on it?"

"No," she replied, "just that there's lots and that it's hot and fresh."

With the order placed, he turned and looked at her. "Now, do you have any contact information for this friend of yours?"

She shrugged. "You won't try to get a hold of him tonight, will you?"

"No, but I'll contact him first thing in the morning."

"I still don't think it's a good idea," she said.

"We have to at least knock him off as a possibility."

Her shoulders sagged. "Fine, but I don't want you terrorizing everybody." She watched his lips twitch.

"How about if I just terrorize the right people?" he murmured.

She had to smile at that. "Okay, I'm all right with that. Yet I doubt that Colby will be anywhere close."

"He may or may not be," Rhys stated, "but better we find out sooner than later."

She agreed with that. "What about Tallahassee?" she asked, looking down at the dog, sprawled out on the floor.

"What about him?" Rhys asked. "He looks to be fairly happy here with you."

"And yet I feel like he's missing something."

"Work. He's been a working dog all his life. He's looking for a job, something to do."

"And protecting me isn't enough?" she asked, as a bit of a joke.

"But he hasn't been with you long enough to understand that that's his job, has he?"

She shrugged. "I don't know. When I got really upset earlier with the shooting," she noted, with a wave of her hand, "he was outside, and, as soon as I let him in, he searched the house top to bottom and then came back and basically just cuddled me."

"Right. Didn't you want him for something like a therapy dog?" he asked.

"I didn't mean it that way," she said. "It was more a case of comfort."

"So a watchdog, a companion?"

She nodded. "Something along that line. So that he could handle himself if things got ugly. So that maybe he would go to bat for me, if nobody else was around. There's nothing like knowing, should you get caught in the middle of the night without your leg, that you can't just run out of the house and defend yourself."

"No," Rhys agreed, "and that always adds to the stress too, doesn't it? My one thought was, what if there's a fire in the middle of the night, and I don't have time to put it on," he added. "I'd get out, but you know that you won't get out anywhere near as well or as fast as somebody with two good legs."

"I know," she agreed. "Those things are stupid thoughts to consider, but they're hard to let go of. I do have a spare crutch that I keep in my bedroom closet but I tend to forget about it."

"Good idea and thoughts like that are hard to let go of because, well, they're a part of who we are now and what we do on a daily basis," he confirmed, "so it's nothing that we need to feel ashamed about."

"And yet," she said, a challenge in her voice, "it's nothing that you don't feel ashamed about either."

He smiled. "I don't think *shame* is quite the right word, but I will agree that it causes stress."

"Exactly," she muttered. "You can stay in the spare bedroom," she offered, her comment coming completely out of the blue.

He stared at her and then nodded. "Thank you."

RHYS WASN'T SURE what brought about that invitation, but he was happy to have it. He could have booked in at a hotel. He'd just let the hotel slide, knowing that a couple bed-and-breakfasts were close by that had vacancies. But he hadn't given it a thought, not wanting to leave her in the condition she was in. Physically she looked like she was doing fine, but the thought of somebody tormenting her drove him crazy with fury. "Do you know where your friend lives?"

She gave him the address, and he wrote it down. Just as he began going through his list of questions, asking her a little bit about timing to make sure that they had everything that they needed, a knock came on her door.

Immediately Tallahassee got up on his back legs, a low growl coming behind his teeth.

Rhys looked over at her. "Does he do this when you order in?"

"I haven't done any ordering in," she stated.

He got up and walked to the door and opened it. It was the pizza guy, but in the background was the same black truck. Rhys paid the delivery guy, gave him a good tip, and asked, "Hey, was that truck here when you pulled in?"

The guy looked at it and nodded. "Yeah, he asked me what I was doing, and I told him that I was delivering pizza."

"Interesting," Rhys noted. "When you leave, can you get me his license plate?"

"Yeah, I guess. I'm parked just across from him, I might be able to."

"And text it to this number." And he pulled out his card and gave it to him.

The guy looked at the card and whistled. "Wow, I don't even know what department that is."

"Don't worry about it," Rhys said. "Just text me when you get it."

"Is he hassling you?"

"Not me, but the woman who lives here alone."

At that, the other man's face screwed up. "That's just messed up."

"Yeah, it is," Rhys confirmed. "That's why I want to know who it is. Somebody did a random drive-by shooting here today."

"You know what? I heard something about that around town. Something about a shooter."

"I don't know for sure that it's him," Rhys stated, ever mindful of not accusing somebody without proof, "but I would like to know who's hanging around."

"You got it," the delivery guy replied enthusiastically, and he pocketed the extra tip. "Thanks, man." And, with that, he stepped out and headed back to his car. He gave a wave to the guy in the vehicle and then carefully drove off.

Probably two minutes later, Rhys got a text. And there was the plate number. With a smile he immediately picked up the phone and then winced. "Damn, I forgot about what time it is."

"What difference does that make?"

"Badger's most likely asleep," he stated.

"Ah," she replied. "I mean, presuming we'll make it through the night, you can contact him in the morning."

But, at her wording, he looked at her and nodded. "You know something? Screw it. I don't like what you just put into words. If Badger's awake, he can find out. If he's not awake, he'll get my text in the morning. But I sure as hell don't want it to be a case of we should have contacted him, and we didn't."

And he quickly sent the license plate with a short explanation to Badger. He got a confirmation almost immediately and a thumbs-up, saying he would run it. Rhys smiled at that. "And look at that. Badger's still awake."

It came back a few minutes later as stolen.

He whistled. "Look at that. The black vehicle out there

is stolen, some two days ago," he shared. "Badger's contacting the police."

"That won't do a whole lot of good either," she muttered. "I don't exactly have a decent rep here."

He quickly texted that to Badger, but his boss didn't give any explanation or any comment. He didn't say anything.

Deciding to take a chance, Rhys phoned Badger. "Hey, I know it's late there, but you're obviously up."

"I am. I'm just looking through my book to see who I can contact."

"Taylor says she hasn't had much luck dealing with anybody here."

"I got that message too," Badger noted. "Don't worry. I'm pretty sure I know somebody decent up there."

"I hope so," Rhys said, "because I'm pretty sure that's the guy who did the drive-by shooting—or at least it's the same truck."

At that, Badger whistled. "We need to get that vehicle off the road, if nothing else."

"And you also know he'll just turn around and steal another one."

"If he stole it, yes, but he may not have," Badger noted. "We'll get to the bottom of it. How's Tallahassee?"

"You know what? I think he's settling in pretty well," he replied, looking over at the dog, even now staring at the pizza box with a voracious hunger that Rhys knew completely made up. "And right now he's trying to coax pizza out of everybody."

"Ha," Badger said, "sounds like he's reverting to a normal dog."

"All of them, when training's over, are exactly that, just a dog."

"No *just* about it," Taylor corrected loyally. "He's a hell of a dog."

"Sounds like Tallahassee found himself a champion," Badger noted.

"Absolutely," Rhys murmured. "A lot of good things to be said about that."

"Agreed. Let's just see if we can solve one problem and then move on to the next."

"Ha, why would we do that," he muttered, "when we could take on all the other problems at the same time?"

At that, Badger laughed. "Jager told me that you were always like that."

"Well, I don't know about *always* like that," he noted, "but injustices drive me nuts."

"Welcome to the club," Badger said. "Welcome to the club."

And, with that, he hung up.

CHAPTER 4

TAYLOR WOKE WITH a start and lay in her bed, wondering where she was and what had just happened. But recognizing her bedroom, she sagged back into the comforter and relaxed. She was home, and, considering the way she felt, she'd gotten some quality sleep. That was a small miracle in itself. She hadn't done well sleeping since her accident. She always had those few nightmares—all about those unresolved issues that she knew perfectly well the shrinks had alluded to, but she had avoided getting into.

Nobody wanted to talk about the problems she'd had before, during, or after any of that military trauma. But to think that now something was rotten in her world here made her even angrier. This was supposed to be her safe space; this was supposed to be a place where she could heal, recuperate, get back to life in some sort of meaningful way. It wasn't supposed to be a place where she was under siege, which is what it felt like.

She thought about the man sleeping in the spare room and about Tallahassee, how she had let him into the house for the first time last night. She was still in an uncertain relationship with the dog, although one that was growing quickly. She'd wanted him to have a few days to get used to being here versus at the shelter. And yet, since she'd been here, it'd been nothing but chaos.

And the fact that Tallahassee had seemed to connect with her so quickly just helped her to realize that she was the one who was more uncomfortable with the dog than the dog with her. But then she hadn't been raised with them all her life, whereas it's obvious that Rhys himself had worked with Tallahassee over the years. She was almost jealous of that. Something was special about a bond with an animal where you knew exactly where you stood and how important it was that you continued on your path for the animal. She'd get there; she knew that.

And to have the dog around was a huge comfort. She'd just been uncertain as to how to handle it. She'd asked the shelter about training opportunities but was also quite aware that the timing was not necessarily something that she would manage easily, not when her leg was still something she had to work with.

She wondered idly if Rhys would spend a few moments and help her out with some elementary dog training tips. He would understand. She'd been more than stunned when she'd seen his prosthetic. And yet why should she? She wasn't the only one missing a limb in this world, no matter how much she tried to make it feel like she was alone and like the world was against her. She wasn't and it wasn't. It just felt like that. And she'd felt alone for a long time now, ever since the military had refused to back her up on the sexual harassment issue.

And knowing that the same asshole was trolling her at home had made her feel even worse. It shouldn't be allowed; there should be some kind of assistance for people like her. And yet, so much of the time, the public assistance from the local cops was for others in more need. Or not even about more in need, just somebody who wasn't in the military.

Maybe because the military supposedly took care of its own? Yet sometimes people, like her, fell through the cracks. Getting taken care of ended up being something completely different than what she had thought it would mean.

It wasn't fair, but, as she'd come to realize, an awful lot in life wasn't fair, and it didn't matter a damn where the hell you fell on that spectrum. You would still get hit with some unfairness at one point in time or another. She got up, and, grabbing her one crutch, hopped her way into the shower, where she had a quick wash. Then she made her way back into her bedroom, where she put on her prosthetic and got dressed.

Afterward she slowly made her way downstairs. She'd hoped not to wake him, only to find him sitting in the kitchen, Tallahassee sprawled at his side. The minute Tallahassee saw her coming down the stairs or heard her, he jumped up and came over to greet her. She gave him a lovely greeting and looked over at Rhys. "Is it okay to have him in the house all the time?"

He looked up with understanding and nodded. "At this point in time he would be a great guard dog, family comfort dog, whatever you need," Rhys explained, "but they definitely like their creature comforts."

She nodded. And then shamefaced she added, "I didn't know. I didn't want to be mean and leave him outside, but, at the same time, I just wasn't sure if it was safe."

"It's safe," he assured her. "As you can see, he's more than happy to see you."

"And what are the chances of him taking over my bed at night?"

At that, Rhys laughed out loud. "Honestly? Probably pretty good," he admitted. "I'm not kidding. They're very much creature comfort dogs at this stage. Not all of them, of course, but, like any dog, he can forget about the kind of training he's had up until now. He's just looking for a place to retire."

"I am too," she agreed bluntly. "I had hoped this was it."

"Is there any reason not to be here?" he asked, looking at her.

"Just the trouble that we've got right now," she stated, unintentionally using a pronoun that included more than just her. He didn't make a comment on it, for which she was grateful. She wasn't sure if she was including him in that or just Tallahassee. She walked over and asked, "You ready for coffee?"

"Absolutely," he said. "I thought about making some earlier, but I didn't want to impose."

She laughed. "It's hardly imposing," she murmured. "Besides, you probably make a better cup than I do."

"I do make a mean cup," he agreed, "but it's your coffee maker. So you'll know it better than I do."

She shrugged and put on the coffee as she always did. "Well, I'm putting it on. If you don't like it ..."

"It'll be fine," he said.

She sat down at the opposite side of the table and asked, "What are you working on?"

"The rundown on the license plate of the vehicle, as well as where it was stolen from," he shared.

"In other words, you're working," she noted, with a wince.

"Sure," he said. "I was awake a while ago, and I didn't want to disturb you. Badger already sent me this information."

"And who is this Badger character?"

"I don't know him as well as I know Jager." Rhys then quickly explained about the team.

She stared at him. "Wow, they sound like they are very together."

"They are. And, if you think they're anything better or different than you, you're wrong," Rhys stated. "All of them are missing limbs, and some of them more than one."

She nodded. "I think one of their best assets is themselves."

"Oh, I agree completely. They have been a team for a long time, so, when one needs help, they're all there for them."

"I had thought, when I was signing up for the military, that I was signing up for a similar type of thing," she murmured. "I didn't expect to be so badly let down."

"And I'm sorry for that," he replied. "It's not what I would have wanted for you either."

She shrugged. "I guess there's just no way to know sometimes, is there?"

"Cases like sexual harassment, sexual assault," he noted, "they're always difficult. Sometimes I'm thoroughly in agreement with how some of these cases work out, and a lot of times I'm not. I have seen both sides of it, where women have called rape—just to get back at some guy—and then where the women were raped and don't even say a word because they're petrified of how they'll get viewed."

"I've certainly seen that too," she murmured. "I just never really thought that, when push came to shove, I would be in the category that got ignored."

"No, I don't imagine anybody ever is," he agreed. "I've also asked for part of your records to see just what might be coming."

"You what?" she asked, staring at him.

He shrugged. "If this harassment issue is related, we need to know all about it."

"You can't just get that though," she stated in shock. And then she looked at him closer. "Or can you?"

"We are all former military, so we have a lot of connections, and I can ask for these records," he explained. "Plus I was sent here initially because you are the guardian of a War Dog, so our welfare checks ensure Tallahassee gets a great retirement situation. Now you've told me more about your personal situation that the military should know about as well. If they are not listening to you, then maybe they'll listen to Badger and to me. So the more you tell me, the easier this investigation will be, both mine and maybe the military's."

"I don't have a problem telling you anything. I have it all down in a file." She shrugged. "I thought I would have to go to a military court over it. Who knew that there wasn't even a case."

He winced at that. "Let me take a look at it."

She shrugged and got up, headed to the far end of the living room, where her desk was, and came back with a file that she dropped on the kitchen table. "This is what I have." She then walked over to the coffeepot that was now done and poured them both some coffee.

"Interesting," he said. "It's pretty thick."

"I collected everything I could—mostly because I was pretty pissed off and fed up with the way I was being treated. And realizing things might go missing, I made sure I had a physical copy as a reference," she declared in a hard tone.

She wanted to see his reaction as he flipped through the file, but she also needed to know what he was looking at too at the time. She couldn't do both, but it didn't really make a difference, as his expression gave away nothing. She'd already been through this file time and time again. She waited as he studied the information.

He nodded. "Sounds pretty standard."

"Sure, it's a she-said/he-said scenario," she stated. "And that never goes well for the woman."

"I don't think it's even so much about the woman as much as it never goes well for the accuser," he clarified. "There are several cases of males being raped as well."

She winced at that. "We never even bring up that particular scenario in life, do we?"

"Very few males will report it," he stated. "Just like you, it doesn't go well for the male accusers either."

"It's a sad world we live in," she said.

"It not completely heartless, but it's definitely got issues." He closed the file, accepted the cup of coffee from her, and asked, "What are your plans for today?"

She shrugged. "Not sure I have any. I probably need to get some more food in the house, from one source or another. Other than that, I'll try to do my exercises and adjust to being home again."

"And yet you've been here for a couple months?"

At that, she nodded. "It sounds as if I should already have my exercises set as a habit, right?" she replied, with a note of humor. "Yet the reality is, I've been to doctors multiple times since I got home, for additional physical therapy, and only just now am I more or less on my own. And I'm still working on setting some sort of a routine."

"Hey, I get it," he said. "I'm a little bit further along than you on some of this but not enough to make a big difference. I have exercises to do as well, especially stretching.

My back's pretty scarred up. I lost a big strip of muscle on it and some tissue. I mean, I tend to wear a shirt all the time, even when swimming, because it scares people."

She raised an eyebrow. "That's not something you need to worry about around me. I don't scare easily." Then she flushed, considering the way sounds set off her PTSD.

"I'll keep that in mind, if it gets hot enough," he replied easily. "What about you? How badly were you injured?"

She nodded, while shrugging. "I was lucky, in one way. I was loading up some big metal pans, reflector sheets," she explained, "at the time of the blast. So that protected me from some of the worst of the accident. The foot, of course, didn't make it, and I've got quite a bit of scar tissue in and around my scalp. I wear my hair a certain way to hide as much of that as I can."

"Well, I didn't notice," he said, "so you're doing a good job there."

She shrugged. "It's a learning process."

"It is, and it's not one that ever goes away," he added. "I went through a whole period where I hated my life and hated everything, but it didn't last long because there's just not enough energy to stay in that wallowing mentality."

"Are you sure?" she asked, with another attempt at humor. "Because sometimes it'd be really nice to just blame the world."

"Maybe for you that works, but it never did for me."

"No, it's not working for me either," she muttered. "Which is why I was thinking that Tallahassee here might be a good addition to my world."

"I think he probably would," Rhys agreed.

"Do you really?" she asked, giving him a sharp look. "Because I don't know anything about dogs."

"And that you can learn," he stated. "You have to come from heart, and, from there, everything else is learnable."

"Learnable and trainable."

"Exactly." He smiled. "And Tallahassee has taken to you quite well."

"Not as well as he's taken to you," she pointed out.

He looked at her steadily. "Does that bother you?"

"Sure, I'd like to know that the dog is loyal to me," she stated. "I don't know that he needs to *only* be loyal to me though."

"Animals will pick and choose those they'll work with, those who they trust, those they like," he told her. "We can force the dogs to work with other people, but then they won't work as well."

She nodded, as she just kept hearing that kind of information to move forward. "So, in other words, this dog might be fine with me and might not."

"I think he'll be just fine with you. The question is whether you can get comfortable enough around him to accept him for who he is."

She stared at him.

"He'll have some of his own issues because of the last few months in his life," he explained. "So you need to accept him too."

"I don't think that's a problem," she muttered. "Lord knows, we probably both need to work on that sense of companionship."

"Exactly," he said.

She looked over at Rhys. "So, if this isn't what you're doing on a regular basis, what do you do normally?"

"I'd say, I'm off to find myself," he shared, "but that sounds trite and makes a mockery out of what I'm really trying to do, which is to figure out my next step, my next career."

"So you don't have a job?"

He shook his head. "I just came out of rehab a couple months ago. Then had gone home to my parents to see about living on my own. Plus I needed to be closer to the prosthetic designer, for her to tweak my newest version," he added. "While I was trying to make some decisions on my future, Jager asked me about coming here to help out with the dog."

"Ah." She nodded. "I was just wondering if you would stay close. If so, then I could ask you for help to train Tallahassee—or to train me."

"I'm not sure that staying close is in the cards," he noted, as he looked around. "Not sure what I'd do here."

"Depends what you're planning on doing."

"Well, I had pretty much written off working with animals for one," he admitted, with a wry look. "At the same time, it is what I know."

"So how about behavior counseling for animals?" she asked, with a laugh.

He looked at her steadily. "I know that that remark was probably made in jest, but there is a need for that."

"Oh my, yes," she agreed, "there absolutely is. I just don't know who all would pay for it."

He shrugged. "No clue. The other thing I could do is train animals, work with therapy animals. I don't know just yet," he admitted. "It's all up in the realm of possibilities."

She hesitated and then asked, "And do you have a decent pension, like I do?"

He nodded. "Most of us have something."

"Something, yes," she noted. "I just don't know how

much of it will be enough."

"Well, thankfully we get medical as well."

"I know," she said, with a nod. "It's funny how, as much as that helps, it's not enough."

"It's never enough," he agreed. "We've lost something major, more than just our respective limbs. We've lost that sense of self, that pride in who we are, that knowledge that we were doing something necessary and needed, and now we're alone, trying to figure out what comes next in our world."

She studied him for a long moment. "No, you're quite right there. It's an odd feeling. I still haven't quite come around."

"I'm a few months ahead of you," he reminded her, "but only a few months."

"I don't know," she murmured. "Feels like you're a lot more than a few months ahead of me."

He nodded. "That's just because you're still at the stage where it feels like the world's gone to shit."

She burst out laughing at that. "Wow, you really do understand, don't you?"

He grinned. "Yes, this kind of stuff I do understand, as do my bosses. As I told you earlier. The team I'm working with now? They've all recovered from major injuries as well."

She nodded. "You know that, to have a group like them, it's a gift."

"Have you looked around locally for something similar for you?"

She shook her head. "I haven't. Cottage Grove is a small town. I could go into the city if I wanted to, but I can't say I want to."

"No, and you're also a private person, who's trying to

keep all this separate, aren't you?"

She smiled. "That is very perceptive of you."

He smiled. "I've been there, done that, so it makes me a little bit more aware of how people like to find ways around what they need to do."

"And you're saying I need to go find a group?" she asked curiously.

"No, I'm definitely not saying that." He looked at her. "But, if you can, find somebody like you."

"Like *you*, you mean," she quipped.

His grin flashed. "As long as I'm here, I am more than happy to help out with the dog and with whatever adjustments you need."

"Yeah, you got an Allen wrench?" she asked. "My leg's killing me."

He looked at her and asked, "Seriously?"

She nodded. "I was supposed to go in and get some adjustments made because this is a temporary one, but things kind of blew up then, and I've got the dog, and I wasn't sure if I was safe going in."

"Let's take a look."

She held up a hand. "After breakfast, I need food first."

He looked at her, smiled, and asked, "Are you always hungry too?"

She nodded. "For the longest time, I didn't want any food, and then, all of a sudden, it's like I can't get full."

"Yeah, I'm more to the point of getting full now," he noted cautiously. "I think our body needs massive fuel to heal us. Anyway I'm always hungry, can always eat."

"Well, I'm not sure what I have here," she admitted, "but I'll find some sort of breakfast in a minute."

"You're not required to look after me," he stated immediately. "I can go to a hotel or a bed-and-breakfast."

"And I'd rather you stayed," she said instantly. And then she hesitated. "Unless you want to leave."

He just smiled and shook his head. "I'm totally good to be here."

She grinned at that. "Well then, let me check out and see what there is for breakfast." And, with that, she got up and headed to the fridge.

Rhys stood too. "Since you're in pain, let me cook. You just rest."

She shook her head. "I know where stuff is and can get this done pretty quickly. It's eggs and toast most likely. Just sit for now."

RHYS WATCHED AS Taylor opened the fridge and took out bacon and eggs, recognizing that her movements were slower, stiffer, not as natural as if she had been walking with her prosthetic for a long time, as he had. Not that he'd been on his for a bigger stretch of time, but he'd gotten a little bit more comfortable with his than she was obviously.

Interested, he asked, "Do you have more surgeries to go?"

She shook her head, as she started cooking the bacon. "No, supposedly everything's fine now. I just need time to adapt."

"And you need to give yourself that time," he agreed, with a nod. "I found it quite difficult at the beginning."

She looked over at him with a wry look. "You don't look like you found it difficult at all," she said. "You're more adjusted than I would ever expect to be."

"And that's not true," he disagreed immediately. "You will find that you do quite well."

"I hope so," she muttered. "It doesn't seem like that right now."

"And I get that, especially in the early stages of adapting to your prosthetic. Plus you have to realize that even a change of prosthetic can make a huge difference too, so speak up to your doc if you're in pain, like now," he suggested, "And don't compare yourself to others. It's always hard to see what looks like other people doing so well, especially when you're not. I've got two months on you. It makes a big difference. Plus I think, in your case, you are doing quite well, but you are expecting too much, too fast. Or you are just naturally hard on yourself. No matter what, give yourself more time and maybe get that prosthetic fixed properly."

"Is it really about giving me more time?" she muttered, looking at him. "It almost feels more like ..." She stopped, hesitated, and then shrugged. "It almost feels like I just ... I haven't quite adapted."

"And there is a huge adaptation process. Eventually you'll realize that you're walking normally and naturally, that you're not shifting to one side, and that it becomes that much easier."

"That's what my hope is," she added, with half a smile. "I'm just not quite there yet."

"And there's no rush either," he noted. "That's something else that you need to just let go of."

She shrugged. "Little hard to do."

"I get it," he said immediately. "I understand. And anytime you want me to shut up, just tell me."

She laughed at that. "No, it's good for me to see you walking around as comfortably as you are. I mean, it's what I hope to get to."

"And you will," he declared. "Give yourself at least two more months down the road. Yet every situation is as individual as each of us are. Remember that."

"And what do you do when it sores up?"

"Get off it immediately," he stated. "Because those sores are deadly, and they're so hard to heal if you don't stop them early."

"It hasn't happened yet," she said. "I was just trying to figure out what to do if and when."

"What you do is immediately get off it," he repeated, with a smile. "You have to understand that sometimes there's nothing you can do. It'll go one way or another, and that's just the way it is."

"Right," she muttered. "Not exactly what I wanted to hear."

"Of course not," he agreed. "And sorry I don't have better news when it comes to that, but really you have to look after your body."

"I get that," she said, "and I'm working on it." And then she laughed. "I didn't mean to get so depressing."

"It's not depressing at all," he noted. "Not a whole lot of people out there have the kind of experiences that we have."

"And that's just what I was thinking of," she shared. "You're so very adapted in a way that you're making it easier for me."

He looked at her and asked, "How's that work?"

"Because I can see that you're okay. So it makes me feel a little bit more like I'm okay."

"Instead of feeling like a freak?"

She winced. "Do you ever feel like that?"

"I did at the beginning, but I was in a rehab center,

where a lot of people were in similar situations," he explained. "So it's only when you get back out into that real world that you start to realize that most people don't have a clue how to adapt to you."

At that, Tallahassee gave a bark, settling in near Taylor at the stove.

Rhys laughed. "I think somebody is trying to tell you that he likes bacon too."

She snorted. "Maybe, when we're done eating, he can have some." Then she grinned. "If you leave him any."

At that, Rhys nodded. "So I still need to know what you're doing today. If you're just staying here, that's fine. I want to go talk to that friend of yours."

"Then I'm coming. That was the conversation we had yesterday," she reminded him. "I do need to come."

"And that's fine. I just want to make sure that we're on the same page. I think we should take Tallahassee with us too."

She nodded. "I don't know how well he travels in a vehicle."

"I've got the rental, and we'll take it," he stated. "How are you doing for driving?"

"Well, it's my left leg, and I have an automatic, and it's, … it's been okay. Having that kind of freedom has been huge."

"Of course it is," he agreed, with a smile. "Just even knowing that you can get back to being *normal* is huge," he said, adding air quotes around the word *normal*.

"That's the thing, you know?" she said. "You don't feel like you're normal."

"And yet you are. You're very normal. It's just you're normal for those of us who have this kind of issue."

"And it, … it doesn't matter whether I wanted it or not," she noted, with a knowing smile. "It's what I've got."

"It's what you've got, and you're doing much better than so many of them."

"And I know that," she replied immediately. "Self-pity was one of the things that I was always trying to avoid."

"I think it's inevitable to feel some self-pity on our way to healing," Rhys noted. "And the fact that you feel it and that everybody tells you that you're not supposed to just makes you feel worse."

She looked at him and said yet again, "You really do understand, don't you?"

"Yes, I do," he stated.

He smiled, when she put a plate of bacon and eggs in front of him, and then he heard the toaster. He hopped up, walked over, grabbed the toast, and came back to the table with it. "As soon as we're done eating, and I take a look at your prosthetic foot, I suggest we call your friend."

"Sure, but I'm not sure calling him ahead of time is a good idea though. He might not want to see me."

"In that case," Rhys decided instantly, "we won't call him. We'll just go visit."

"And if he's not there?"

"We'll try again later," he said, with a smile. "And I do want to know what's happening with this other guy from the military that you accused. I've got calls in about that too."

"I haven't seen him around town," she noted, "so I can't imagine that it's him."

"Doesn't mean he didn't hire somebody to come torment you."

She stared at him. "Well, that certainly would give me pause. I hadn't considered that."

"Does he have money?"

"His parents do, yes," she stated. "But what good would it do?"

"Depends whether there's still a tribunal investigating. In which case anything this guy can do to try to make it look like you're mentally unstable, it could throw out your testimony."

She just stared at Rhys and then down at her plate, before picking up a piece of bacon and popping it into her mouth. "I would have thought there was absolutely nothing left that they were even looking at," she said. "So I don't know if that's valid or not, but it would be nice to think that they were still looking into my case."

"Why don't we go on the assumption that this asshole still considers you a threat?"

She winced at that. "I was hardly a threat back then," she noted, "so I don't really see that anybody will consider me a threat now."

"And we don't know that," Rhys stated calmly. "We'll go find out and make sure he's not this gun-happy jerk who's been shooting at your place. Did you end up calling the cops?"

She hesitated, then shook her head. "No."

"Okay, so now I need to know why."

"Why is simple—because they don't give a crap."

"Have you called them before?"

"Sure," she said, "they didn't give a crap then either."

"And what was it about?"

"I was pretty sure that I had an intruder in the house. This was when I first moved back in here," she replied, with a heavy sigh, sitting back and looking at him. "They didn't find anything, didn't find anyone, and I had had a couple drinks. No, I wasn't drunk. I wasn't even close to it," she stated bitterly. "But believe me, my reputation took a hit."

"Any particular reason?"

"Yeah, because this guy Andrew, who we will go see, his uncle works in the police station."

"And you think he gave you a bad rap?"

"I don't know what he did," she said. "I just know it all went to pot really fast."

"Good enough. We will go check it out, and I know that Badger's looking for somebody we can trust in the sheriff's office."

"You mean somebody who's unbiased?" She shook her head. "Maybe I should move, just so that people don't know who I am."

"It doesn't matter who you are," he stated. "You deserve the same treatment as everyone else."

She gave him a look. "You really are an innocent, aren't you?"

He burst out laughing. "No, but I do believe that justice is for everyone and not just for the people who believe in it."

"Well then, you need to know that I have a bit of history here as well," she admitted. "My parents were alcoholics and fought all the time, so there were a lot of domestic abuse calls coming from our house. They are both MIA now, which is fine with me."

"And what does your parents' alcoholic marriage mean to anybody now?"

"I don't know. I'm sure there's a file on it. Maybe they think I'm just as crazy as my mother."

"And was there domestic abuse?"

"You know what? There probably was," she noted, with a heavy sigh. "But I'm not sure who was abusing who." He stared at her, and she just shrugged. "They both drank. They both screamed and hollered, and she usually called because my dad wouldn't ever call, and that would be no good for his ego, I'm sure," she explained in a wry tone. "At the same time, I think the police department just labeled all of us as nuts."

"Which has nothing to do with where you're at now. When they came and checked out because you had an intruder, what did they say?"

"I think once they realized the address and who it was, I was dismissed."

"Which is not their right to do," he said, his voice hard.

"Maybe not, but, as I told you, I'd had a couple drinks. I was feeling pretty shitty at the time. I was hoping that maybe it would help with the pain. But instead it, … it didn't, and it made things way worse for me. I haven't had a drink since."

"We're all entitled to have a drink to relax in the evening," he said, "at any time of the day, if we're in our own home and not driving. This is your life."

She gave him half a smile. "It might be my life, but it certainly feels like I'm not the one dictating it."

"Well, that'll change now," he declared, with a promise that he meant to keep. "I don't like anybody getting slotted into being something that they aren't just because of their history."

"Maybe not," she agreed, "but you can't always dictate how everybody else looks at your life."

"Maybe not," he muttered equally fast. "But it also doesn't mean that they get to judge you for your history."

"Are you kidding?" she asked, with a laugh. "That's all people do—is judge."

He winced at that. "Maybe, but that doesn't mean that they'll continue to do it now."

She shook her head. "You're back to that Pollyanna attitude again now."

He smiled. "Maybe. Finish up your breakfast, down the coffee, so I can look at your foot. Then we're going to see Andrew."

CHAPTER 5

TAYLOR WALKED OUT to the vehicle Rhys had rented and smiled when she saw it was a truck. "Is there anything guys like better than your trucks?" she teased.

"I don't know," Rhys said, with a big grin. "I always prefer to rent one if I can."

"Of course you do. It's not as if you need a truck here though."

"Nope, but it feels better," he noted. "It's what I'm used to driving, and it's what I'm comfortable with. And I'm not exactly a small guy."

She realized that because she was tall herself, and she didn't really compute just how tall he was. "And it's funny that I always think of tall guys as normal."

"I do too because that's what I am. But the world of vehicles isn't always as easily accessible for us."

She nodded. "My dad's six foot six."

"You come by it honestly then, don't you?"

"I sure do. My mom's five-ten."

"Wow, so no wonder you're ... what? Close to six-foot?"

She shrugged. "About five-eleven." Then she looked down at her leg and added, "Well, I was."

"You still are," he replied immediately. "Even standing on one leg. Interesting that you've got the bulk of your leg. I'm missing mine higher up."

"I was told, when I first lost it, that I was lucky."

He laughed. "Don't you hate it when they shove that crap down your throat?"

She looked at him, and her smile was spontaneous and real. "Exactly. They just don't get it. I'm tired of people telling me how I'm lucky. I get it. I'm lucky in that I'm lucky to be alive. I'm lucky about a lot of things, but, until I adjust and deal with my new life," she explained, "having people constantly tell me that I'm lucky to be alive is not what I want to hear."

"Ditto," he said. "Now let's go visit your friend."

She hopped up into the vehicle and noted that Tallahassee was already in the back seat, waiting for them. "He seems to be quite happy traveling in a vehicle," she marveled.

"He should have done lots of it in the military, but most of it would have been crated," Rhys added. "Yet a lot of dogs are good travelers. Some aren't though, so, in this case, we'll find out how Tallahassee is now." And, with that, Rhys started up the vehicle, turned to her, and asked, "Where are we going?"

"Oh, right." She frowned as she looked around, wondering at the best way to go, and then she quickly gave him directions to get started. "I really haven't seen him in quite a while."

"So this would be just like Old Home Week."

She groaned. "I don't know what kind of reception we'll get."

"Well, if he's involved, not a good one."

"I can't imagine him being involved," she muttered, "but I don't know."

"You said you all were friends at the time when the four of you enlisted. And Andrew and the jerk still are?"

"Sure, but that doesn't mean that all our friends go out and do stuff like drive-by shootings and shit."

"No, but Andrew might know about it, or he might suspect it. Either way, it'll make him less comfortable, once he realizes that we're potentially looking at him."

"But are we looking at Andrew?" she asked.

"I'm looking at anybody and everyone," he stated, turning to glance at her. "And so should you."

She winced at that. "I'd just as soon not look at anyone."

"And sticking your head in the sand, does that work for you?"

"Of course not," she replied in exasperation and then realized he was teasing her. "You know what? As much as I hate to say it, you're probably good for me."

He looked at her. "Why?"

"Because you don't let me hide at home. You're forcing me to go out and to think differently. I have done much less outside than I've done inside. I've been hiding, I guess."

"Well, hiding is what we do," he stated, "until we're comfortable to go out and to deal with the stares. At least you have a prosthetic, so the stares should be minimal."

"They are now," she noted. "But, when I first got here, I didn't have one yet. So, between the crutches and the generic prosthetics, which aren't minimal in size, I felt like I always got branded right from the beginning."

"That's just people. Most of the time it's honest curiosity instead of being an outright asshole. And you do know, for anybody who's not seen people with prosthetics, the first time is a bit of an eye-opener."

"It just wasn't an eye-opener that I really wanted to give my local community."

He grinned at that. "Well, looks like you're a little too

late for that because it sounds like you already did."

"I guess. I just …" Then she stopped, shrugged, and added, "I know it's foolish. I shouldn't give a crap."

"None of us should," Rhys agreed, "but we're human, and what we're dealing with is all too human as well. So give yourself a break and understand that there'll be people who stare and that there'll be people who don't have a clue, and we're not concerned about any of them."

And, with that, she settled back and continued to give him directions to get where they were going.

By the time they pulled up in front of Andrew's place, she sighed. "Haven't been here in a long time, but it looks just the same."

"Is that good or bad?"

"In my world it's good," she replied. "We used to be friends. We used to pick up Chinese food at midnight and take it down to the waterways and just relax. There's such a, … I don't know, *comfort* in seeing something that's timeless."

"Good," he noted. "Let's see if we can find more things that are timeless for you."

"Like what?" she asked.

"Friendship." And, with that, he hopped out of the vehicle and let Tallahassee out too.

She followed, slower, wondering at how well he seemed to get her and to understand what was going on in his world versus her world. She sighed. "I know you probably don't want to hear this, but, if you feel like hanging around town longer, I could use a friend."

He looked at her, and then a big grin flashed. "You know something? That's the nicest invitation I've heard in a long time."

"Well, don't be too happy," she stated, her tone turning caustic, as she realized that she'd probably shared way too much. "I was just feeling alone."

"Of course you are," he noted, a bounce to his step as he walked over and hooked his arm through hers. "Come on. Let's go see what this Andrew guy's got to say for himself."

RHYS SNAPPED THE leash on Tallahassee, handed Taylor the leash, and said, "No time like the present."

Nervously she took the leash. Tallahassee didn't seem to care; his tail was wagging like a crazy man, just happy to be out on a road trip. She had to wonder. "I used to love going for car rides," she murmured. "This is the first time I've really been out of the house to do anything since arriving here."

"And that's too bad," he declared. "When we've lost as much as we have, I think it's important to honor the bits and pieces that we have left."

She chuckled. "I get that. I really do. But along with that previous life was friends to do any activity with. And I guess maybe what I'm feeling is just ..." She stopped, hesitated, and then said, "Lonely."

He looked at her, smiled. "And I understand that too. I lost a lot of friends afterward. I lost a lot of friends in the military, in the navy. They weren't blown up to bits and didn't get medically discharged. I did. Our lives have taken a massive divergence right now, and it's hard to see whether we'll get beyond that or not," Rhys stated. "Obviously I'd like to maintain the same friendships I had, but I'm not sure that I can. They're already off on missions that they can't talk about, and I can't do anything but wish I was there."

"Ouch. And I'm totally okay to miss the supply line assignment," she said, chuckling. "That was never all that exciting."

He smiled. "No, and the things that you do keep are the things that are really important to you, but right now what's important is that you build slowly, and then, when you have enough inside yourself, you'll step out of your comfort zone, and you'll do a little bit more."

"Promise?" she asked, with a laugh.

"I do promise," he stated, with a smile. "I think we just tend to forget that we have to take this in stages."

"And how did you get to be so wise?" she asked in exasperation, as they walked up to the front of Andrew's house.

"I don't know," he replied. "I mean, honestly I think it's just something that you learn or you don't learn, as you go through life, and I also think that it helps to have somebody else with you. I had friends in the VA centers. I think, in that case, you probably had it harder."

"Well, I had people there. At that point in time I was already pretty …" She hesitated and then added, "doubting, untrustful, struggling to believe anybody would be there for me or that they …"

"Wouldn't betray you?"

She winced. "Am I really so obvious?"

"No. But given what's happened," he stated, "I can imagine that trusting anyone would become a huge issue for you. And when you're in a VA center like that, where you're already dealing with other people who are broken and dealing with their own problems, it's pretty common to bundle up and to just become almost a stranger to the world around you."

"I did everything I needed to do," she explained. "I put in all the effort that I could. But you're right. It felt like everybody around me would betray me, so I didn't talk. I didn't visit. I did my crap, and, as soon as I was discharged, I came home." She shook her head. "I have zero contact with anybody. And I think that was a mistake."

"I'm not sure that it's a mistake, as much as it was life at the time," he noted. "So stop trashing yourself for being human and give yourself a pass for doing the best you could in the circumstances. Now come on. Let's go talk to this *friend* of yours."

"Yeah, and, trouble is, now I don't know who's a friend and who's a foe anymore."

"Let's go find out." Rhys walked toward the door, their arms still linked, not dragging her but not letting her slow down either.

"You walk much faster than I do," she muttered.

"That's because you're still trying to find your way," he said, "whereas I'm pretty confident in my legs."

"Yeah, ... I need to get back into the gym, but with the prosthetic"—she shrugged—"I've really ... It's been in the back of my mind, but I just haven't mentally managed to get myself there."

"And you'll need to find the right person to be your training partner," he added, with a smile. "Because the wrong person will send you back into hiding."

She winced at that. As they reached the front door, she sighed, reached out, and knocked. When there was no answer, she looked at Rhys and shrugged. He reached out and, with a tight fist, pounded hard. She stared at him. "So, if he's still asleep, you're trying to drag him out of bed?"

"I just want to make sure that he knows it's not some

gentle little knock out here and that somebody wants to talk to him."

"Doesn't mean that there'll be anybody inside who wants to talk to you," she reminded him.

The door opened at that, and a sleepy Andrew stared from her to him, before wiping the sleep out of his eyes. "What's with the pounding?" he asked in a mild-enough tone.

"Just want to make sure that somebody was home and awake," Rhys answered.

The guy stared at him. "I don't know you." He looked over at her and said, "Hey, what's up?"

She didn't know whether he'd had a chance to couch his expression or not, but he didn't seem to be terribly upset or surprised to see her. She shrugged. "We got a spot of trouble that we need to ask you some questions about."

His eyebrows shot up again. "Trouble? Why the hell would you even come to me with something like that?"

Rhys searched for lies in Andrew's tone, but it seemed honest, at least for the moment. At that, Rhys turned to him and asked, "Can we come in?"

Andrew didn't like that request, but he looked around first and then said, "Sure, I guess." Yet he didn't move. He looked back at Taylor. "Jesus, Taylor. What's going on?"

She shrugged. "This is Rhys from the War Dogs department."

"War Dogs? What the hell?" he asked, looking even more confused.

She shrugged. "If you let us in, we could explain."

And Andrew immediately stepped back. "Sure. Whatever. Come on in. It's not like I would get any more sleep anyway."

And just enough exasperation filled his voice that she winced. "Yeah, I wondered if we should have waited until later."

"Yeah, you should have," Andrew agreed, "at least until I was awake."

"And when would that be?" she asked, with a note of humor. "You're well known for sleeping till noon."

"So afternoon would have been sensible," he stated, but his tone had lightened. As they walked inside, Andrew led the way to the kitchen and said, "I don't know about you, but I need coffee. And, if you're planning to ask me any questions, I'll need a couple cups."

As soon as he put on the coffee, he turned, leaned against the counter, his hands at his back, and stared at her. "You look good."

Rhys noted just enough surprise in Andrew's voice that she must have looked pretty crappy before.

"I'm doing much better," she said immediately.

"Good, I'm glad to hear that."

This time Rhys heard potentially some honesty in Andrew's tone. Enough to give Andrew a slight pass on it anyway.

Andrew looked over at Rhys, held out his hand, and said, "I'm Andrew. I presume you already know that she and I were in elementary school through graduation together."

"Yep, I do know," Rhys replied, with a grin. "Relationships like that tend to count when you get older."

"I don't know why," Andrew stated. "I sure as hell haven't had anything to do with her for a long time, so pardon me if this visit comes out of the blue." He looked down at the dog. "I didn't even know the dog was with you two. Is this your dog?" he asked, confused, as he looked over at her.

"I didn't know you had a dog."

"He's a new member of the family," she murmured, reaching out a hand to Tallahassee.

Rhys was happy to see that Tallahassee had absolutely no compunction about stepping forward and shoving his nose into her hand. The War Dog turned and looked at Andrew, but the dog offered him no such welcome—almost as if Tallahassee were withholding judgment.

"I don't think he likes me," Andrew said in a harder tone. "He better not be dangerous."

"He's not dangerous," Rhys replied immediately. "He's a very well-trained War Dog."

"What the hell's a War Dog even?" Andrew asked in exasperation. "Unlike her and possibly you," he noted, with a frown, "I don't have very much military training."

"That's a lie," she disagreed hotly. "You just went out early."

"Yeah, I did my five years, and I was gone," he confirmed. "Enough was enough of that shit. You know that we went into the army young and stupid, and some of us got out before ..." And he waved at her leg.

"Yeah," she said, "I get that. I'm out now anyway."

"Sure you are, but, Jesus, you're missing a body part or two." He shook his head. "Why didn't you listen to me? You could have come out with me at the time."

"Well, if I'd realized what would happen in my future," she replied, "maybe I would have, but hindsight being 20/20, I didn't have any of that advanced knowledge." Her own irritation rose. "And, sure, obviously I would like anything to have happened that would have avoided me losing a foot, but this is what I have for cards to deal with."

He shrugged. "I get it, and you were always one of those

patriotic do-gooders."

"I'm not sure why you went into the military if you weren't one too."

"I don't know why," Andrew said in exasperation, snapping at her. "Honest to God, I blame you and Colby for filling my head with that romantic BS."

"And yet you got out of the army, so it's not a problem now," she noted, sharing a frown with Rhys.

Rhys gave her a slight nod, wondering at Andrew's aggression, like she probably was too.

Andrew shrugged. "Sure. And, in the end, it makes me feel guilty as hell. I got out with a life, and I know I was the one who made the right decision, but you wouldn't listen to me. And now that you finally came back, at least you didn't come in a pine box," he snapped. "God, that would be terrible."

"Yeah, not that I would have cared a whole lot at that point in time," she added, with mild amusement. "But coming back in pieces? Well, that was much harder for me."

He raised both hands. "Dammit, why didn't you just listen to me?"

"Because apparently I needed to do what I thought was right," she said, her voice calm.

At those words, Rhys looked at her with admiration, before addressing Andrew. "Just because she lost a leg, she's no less than she was before."

"Maybe not," Andrew grumbled, "but she could still be whole."

"She's whole in so many other ways," Rhys noted. "I don't really see that this is a healthy conversation for her."

The guy looked at Rhys and snapped, "Maybe not, but it's an overdue conversation." He looked over at her, and she nodded.

"Absolutely it's overdue," she agreed. "I gather you'd like us to leave."

"Hell yes. Just seeing you makes me angry."

She smiled. "And maybe that's true. Maybe all this is just something that pisses you right off, but it's Colby I want to ask you about."

At that, his eyebrows shot up. "What about him? He wouldn't listen either. Jesus Christ, it still makes me so angry." He walked over to the coffee, poured himself a big cup, and then turned and asked, "You guys want some?"

She immediately nodded. "Yes, please."

Rhys smiled. "Sure, I'll have a cup. When did you last see Colby?"

He banged the cups down on the table, full of coffee now, and glared down at Rhys. "What the hell is it to you?"

Rhys looked over at her and asked, "How much do you want to tell him?"

She winced. "Not a hell of a lot."

"Yeah, *not a hell of a lot*. And that's what I'm getting from this message. Now screw off. If you won't tell me what the hell's going on, I won't have anything to do with you either." He glared at her. "We've been friends for a shit ton. What the hell's going on now?"

She sighed. "You won't believe it."

"Well, that may be, but I think you're too far into whatever the hell nightmare you're into," he stated, "for me to sit here and to tell you anything, *until you talk*."

She looked over at Rhys, shrugged, and said, "Fine."

CHAPTER 6

TAYLOR STARED DOWN at the coffee, figuring out how to even tell Andrew.

He got impatient and snapped, "Come on. Just spit it out."

"Fine," she snapped right back. "Have you had any conversations with Colby in the last year or so?"

"Sure I have," he said, "but not a lot. The man's ..." He stopped, hesitated, then shrugged. "Let's just say, he's changed."

"Yeah, he has." She winced, looked at Rhys. Then addressed Andrew again. "I don't know if Colby mentioned me at all."

Andrew nodded. "Told me that you were playing hard to get."

"Hell no," she spat. "I never had any intention of going out with him in the first place."

"I don't know why he would think that you would," Andrew muttered. "You never gave him any indication that I knew of all these years we've known each other."

"Exactly," she muttered. "And then in the military ..." She took a deep breath and began, "You might find this a little hard to believe."

Andrew shrugged. "Maybe, definitely a different interpretation in a lot of things has been going on, but I won't have a clue what to say until I hear the whole story."

And, with that, she launched into an explanation of what happened. Andrew made several noises as she went on, but she plowed forward, not sure whether she would have the guts to continue her story if she stopped. When she finally did, Andrew stared at her for a long moment or two, then got up, pacing the kitchen.

"Good God," he said, "are you sure?"

She raised an eyebrow.

"Right, of course you're sure. Crap." He ran his hand over his face. "I don't even know what to say to that."

"It'd be nice if you believe me," she stated, a certain bitterness in her voice. "I'm sure you can imagine how the military viewed it."

He winced at that. "You're right about that. I can't say that I necessarily like the way that the military treated women," he noted. "It was pretty rough on a lot of people, and I know that their process isn't the easiest to go through either. Yet I can hardly … see him doing something like that." He rushed in to explain. "It just seems so foreign to me."

"And me," she agreed. "It's not how I expected him to treat me either."

At that, Andrew stopped his pacing and sat down at the kitchen table. "Good God. That's still, I mean, even though it's a shit story to come here and tell me about because we three were friends, and we are *still* friends. However, in spite of whatever I'm hearing right now, I don't have any reason at the moment to *not* be his friend, but that doesn't explain why you're here."

She frowned, then said, "If you're Colby's friend, after hearing what I just told you, then you and I can't be friends." She glanced over at Rhys and said, "You need to take this over." Rhys nodded. And, while she listened and sipped her coffee, Rhys brought Andrew up to date on the shooting at her house, the earlier break-in, all attempts to possibly make it look like she was losing it.

At that, he stared in shock. "Seriously? But that's just a shit thing to do."

"I know," she agreed, a wry tone to her voice, "which is part of the problem."

He sat back. "I … I don't even know what to say."

She nodded but didn't say anything because, well, what was she supposed to say at this point? If Andrew didn't believe her, then he didn't believe her, and nothing had really changed by telling him her story. It was a fact of life that not necessarily everything went your way. Still, she found it so odd that Andrew had a problem with the way the military handled women—since he was treating her just like the military did, with disbelief.

Regardless, she could write off this *friend*. She also wasn't sure if they were ever really friends. A lot of time and energy had gone by the wayside supporting that pseudo-relationship. She could hardly believe he took Colby's side, after he had noted how Colby had changed before she had even shared her additional facts with Andrew.

He sat back and muttered, "Shit."

"Yeah, that's one way to look at it," she noted, with a smirk.

He stared at her. "Is that why I haven't heard from you since you got back?"

She shrugged. "Partly, yes. Partly I was still adjusting to the leg." She didn't remind him that he crossed the street whenever he saw her. If he wanted to hope she hadn't seen him, she'd let him.

He looked down at her leg and frowned. "And that still just pisses me right off, and I guess that's why I didn't call you. A part of me wants to smack the hell out of you for not having followed my lead and gotten out of there."

She snorted. "The last time you did that, I think I was about eight."

"Yeah, and you kicked my ass afterward."

Such affection was in his tone that she had to laugh. "Now that's very true," she admitted. "And I know a lot of time has passed between those good old days and now. I wouldn't be here except for Rhys."

"That doesn't make me feel any better," he stated in disgust, looking at her. "What am I supposed to do with that?"

"Understand why—from my point of view for a change," she said bluntly. "And hopefully understand that where I've been to and where I need to go is still a distance."

He nodded in understanding. "But that doesn't mean you have to do it alone."

"That's something I just told her too," Rhys added, chuckling, "but she doesn't necessarily follow advice."

At that, Andrew gave a hard snort. "No, she doesn't. Otherwise she would have saved herself a lot of this trauma."

"Maybe," she replied, "and maybe not. Some things we just have to learn to do ourselves."

He nodded at that. "I get you there," he murmured. "It still sucks though."

She smiled. "At least you didn't jump up and flat-out tell me that I'm lying."

"Hell no, I wouldn't do that. Am I struggling with it? Yes. I absolutely am struggling with it. I know Colby can be a shit, but I didn't think he was that big a shit." He paused, frowning. "And the military? Well, you know I didn't have a great experience there. I couldn't wait to get out, so I'm not surprised that that was their reaction. The higher-ups definitely favor the males, and it doesn't know how to handle any sexual harassment, much less assaults. Other than, you know, you're supposed to keep your legs closed kind of stuff."

"I know all that," she stated, "and I presume that my case was closed, that basically nothing would be done about it, so I don't understand why Colby would be coming after me or sending someone after me if that were the case."

"I hate to say it," Andrew began, looking at Rhys and then back at her. "But I'll just come out and ask it. Is there any chance that you might have misunderstood?"

"Misunderstood somebody's shooting into her house?" Rhys asked, his tone hard. "It's not just her who's saying that. I'm a witness to it, and I'm saying that."

At that, Andrew winced. "Right. And you would just love a chance to kick my ass for doubting her too."

"No, not so much. Sounds like she can do that herself," Rhys noted. "You were friends before, so I think she's giving you too much benefit of a doubt here. Even so, she's finding out if there's any reason left to be friends with you."

Andrew stared at the two of them. "Just because I don't like anything that you've had to say since you got here doesn't mean I'll call you a liar," he stated. "I don't know what the truth is about what's going on in your world. I hope you're wrong. Am I surprised? Am I shocked? Not necessarily. Do I really hope that Colby has nothing to do with this shit? Yes, of course I do. Partly because I don't want to believe he's that kind of a guy. And yet another part of me …" He stopped and hesitated and then added, "I know he's fully capable of it."

She leaned forward and asked, "What?"

He shrugged. "He's always been pretty aggressive as a male. Whether you saw that or not? I guess maybe you didn't."

"I certainly saw it once we were in the military, and something about that rah-rah stuff made him get a little bit more so," she noted. "It wasn't to his advantage."

"No, I don't imagine it was," Andrew agreed. "And honestly you know a lot of good things can be said about him. Like, for example, he's definitely there for you, if you need a friend. Yet he's also got some hard edges. And maybe the military exaggerated that."

"Exactly. I know so. He got very …" She shrugged. "I don't even know how to say it. He got more aggressive from it. As if he were *the man*."

"And, in his mind, he would be the man," Andrew noted. "He would be the one who would be the boss. He would know more than you, be better than you, and, if you weren't cooperative, he probably wouldn't have asked for permission. Hate to say it, but some changes in him I didn't like. Something that the military never talks about."

Rhys got to his feet and asked Andrew, "Would you mind if I took the dog out back for a moment?"

He looked at him and shook his head. "No, go for it, man. I guess the dog has to lift a leg sometime, doesn't he?" He stared at the dog and asked, "Is this one of the War Dogs?"

Rhys nodded. "Yes, Taylor ended up finding him at a shelter. We were notified that there was a problem and came down to help her out."

"Wow," Andrew said. "How come nobody helped her

out when she was in the military?"

"I was in the navy," Rhys clarified, "so I can't answer that particular question as it pertains to the army, but it's a valid one." At that, he turned and led the dog out the back door.

As soon as Rhys left, Andrew turned and faced her. "What the hell?" he said. "Why the hell are you even here now? I don't even know what to think, but this isn't the shit I wanted brought to my door."

She stared at him, then snidely replied, "I'm so sorry that my temporary and permanent problems may cause you some discomfort for a few hours, then you can just go back to your regularly scheduled life." She paused, then answered his question directly. "I needed to know if you knew where Colby was and if you thought he was capable of this."

"He's male," Andrew stated bluntly. "That means he's capable. Is he unhinged to the extent that he would do something like this? I have no idea." Andrew shook his head. "I don't even know what to think about any of it." And then he reached up and rubbed his face. "Man, if you'd let me have another six hours of sleep, it would have helped."

She laughed. "Next time we'll consider it."

"Yeah, well, make sure next time you aren't bringing shit to my door either. Fuck, I don't want to deal with this now." He looked outside and asked, "Now what's he doing?"

She hopped her feet, walked over to the window, and looked out. "I'm not sure, but the dog appears to have led him there."

"*Great*," he muttered, an odd note to his tone. "When he gets back, take off, will ya?"

She nodded. "Will do. Wouldn't want to disturb you for thirty minutes out of the rest of your life."

"Look. I'm being a jerk. I know it. You know it. That guy knows it," Andrew admitted. "What the hell am I supposed to say to Colby when he calls me?"

"I don't know," she replied. "Don't have a clue. I don't even know what to say to you now."

He just glared at her.

That was his way. He'd always been that way—somebody who didn't want to get involved. "I know you don't like this kind of shit visiting your door, but, considering people are shooting at me, and I'm no longer even in the service," she explained, "I needed to know."

"Needed to know what?" he asked, throwing up his hands.

The rear screen door opened, and Rhys replied, "If you've had any contact with Colby, if he said anything about what he's up to, and if you think he'd try to kill her."

"Like that's easy ..." Andrew grumbled. "Any other questions you want to ask?"

RHYS STARED AT the man. He was still of two minds, trying to decide if Andrew was helping or hurting their case. Since Rhys had come back inside, an odd silence ensued. The fact that Andrew had at least listened was good, but now it seemed like he was chewing on the whole issue—not so much with doubt but with disdain.

Taylor looked over at Rhys. "Andrew's always prided himself on staying out of other people's affairs and not getting into trouble."

"That's a nice life if you can get it," Rhys stated. "It doesn't always work out for everybody though."

"And yet it should," Andrew disagreed almost bitterly. "I don't even know how I'm supposed to react right now."

At that, Rhys looked at him. "Truthfully would be a good start."

"I get it. She's upset, and all this shit has been going down, and I didn't know anything about it, until now—and, for that, I'm sorry because, well, that's just a shit deal for anybody to go through. The accident, the injury, somebody coming to your place and shooting it up, that is just, … that is just a shitty move on anybody's part," he muttered. "But you're telling me that one of my best friends is responsible, … and that I really struggle with."

"I'm not telling you that he's responsible, directly or indirectly. At least that wasn't what I was trying to tell you," she murmured. "I was trying to see if you had any idea what he's capable of, if you've seen him in town recently, if you know anything about what he's up to currently."

"And yet all it sounded like was you were dishing dirt on him."

She stared at him, and Rhys felt her start to withdraw. Her benefit of the doubt had just expired. "I hardly think *dishing dirt* after what she's been through is quite the right turn of phrase," Rhys said, his voice hard. "Somebody is trying to stop her from doing something. I don't know what the hell this Colby guy's deal is or why, but, if you see him around, tell him that I want to talk to him," Rhys snapped, as he walked over and gave her a hand up. "Time for us to go." She stood. Rhys nodded at Andrew. "Your *friend* here needs to decide which side of this he's on."

"What do you mean?" Andrew asked.

"When the chips fall," Rhys declared, "they won't fall evenly. A coin only lands on one side or the other. You'll

have to decide which side of that coin you're falling on."
And, with that, he led her out the front door. He was so
angry the shudders rippled through him.

"Are you all right?" she asked, as they stepped outside.

He nodded. "I'm all right, but you need new friends."

She sighed. "Like I said, I wasn't a big fan of coming
here in the first place."

"No, but you had to sow the seeds, and Andrew will do
whatever he does. I mean, he obviously didn't care about
being a patriot for the sake of helping his country, so I'm not
sure he'll give a crap about helping you either. When your
buddy Colby calls Andrew," Rhys added, "he'll be put on the
spot one way or another. I just don't know which way he'll
jump when that particular coin falls."

He helped her into the vehicle, turned on the engine,
and with Tallahassee in the back, she said, "I don't understand what's going on right now."

He looked over at her, his eyebrows raised.

She continued. "You came back inside really fast with
Tallahassee. What was going on?" And then she noted the
dog was alert, searching around them. "Oh my God, did you
see something out there?"

"Not so much that *I* saw something out there, but Tallahassee did. And believe me. I didn't want to stick around
long enough to see exactly what or who it was."

She stared at him in shock. "Are you saying Andrew's
involved?"

Rhys shook his head, hearing her heart breaking at the
idea. "I'm not saying anything definitive yet, except for the
fact that somebody was watching the place. And I don't even
know if your *friend* knows it."

"Maybe we should tell him?"

"No, I'm not up for that. Your friend's got his own life that he's determined to lead independently of whatever you've got going on," he explained. "And that'll be a telling point coming up too."

She stared at him. "But if he's in danger?"

"Well, that's the question," he noted, as he took a corner hard. "What I want to do is see who is behind his place, but I needed to make sure that you wouldn't be a sitting duck. So, as far as I'm concerned, we'll go take a drive right now and see what I can find. It was all I could do to keep Tallahassee quiet, and, if not for his training, you can bet that he would have let out a warning while we were in the backyard."

She stared down at the dog, who even now had his head between Rhys and the window. "Does he know what we're doing?"

"Oh, yeah," Rhys confirmed. "This is a hunting dog. He's just not necessarily sure what the prey is." And Rhys quickly took another corner and then held up a finger and said, "Now be quiet."

And he shut off the engine. With that, he slipped out, Tallahassee at his side, as both disappeared from Taylor's view. She stared in shock, wondering if she was supposed to follow. He had told her to stay quiet; he didn't say, *Stay in the vehicle.* She slipped out of the vehicle and moved slowly toward where maybe Andrew's property was, just from the back access.

She had no clue where she was, but obviously Rhys had some idea. Her sense of navigation had never been great, but she didn't think it was as bad as it was right now. She looked around the area, trying to get her bearings, but she was only a block away from Andrew's house. Even as she stood here and watched for something, for anything, she caught sight of Andrew on the far side. He stood out on his deck, phone in hand. And her heart sank.

"What are the chances," she whispered out loud, "that you're phoning that asshole."

Now it didn't mean that Andrew was phoning Colby and saying, *Watch out. They're after you.* It could also be *What the hell's going on. I just heard a terrible story.* At least that's the way she wanted it to play out in her mind. But she hadn't been born yesterday, and the one thing Rhys had told her that was to be her focus was that she must be constantly looking to see who else would betray her in this new world that she no longer knew or understood. It broke her heart to realize that just so many shitty people were out in this world, and somehow she had gotten caught up with at least one of them. With a hard sigh, she watched as Andrew put away his phone and then headed deeper into the back portion of his property.

With her eyes now wide, she watched as he stepped over into the neighbor's yard and then came around again. She quickly dashed to stand behind the truck, as Andrew came toward where she was, but then Andrew dodged to another corner and disappeared from sight. Now curious and wondering what the hell was going on, she headed after Andrew, wondering if Rhys was right. Maybe Andrew was helping Colby get away with this shit. Because, if Colby had an alibi, then of course it would make her look even more delusional.

Her heart sinking, she quickly crept through the trees, so that she could get a better view. When Andrew stepped forward and took a look around, as if looking for somebody, she watched as another vehicle drove up. She didn't recognize who was in the vehicle, but she watched as Andrew argued with somebody inside the vehicle. And then, just like that, the argument ended. Andrew raised both hands in mock surrender, got inside the vehicle, and they drove off.

It was all she could do to grab enough wits about her to write down the license plate. She had no idea what the hell just went down, but, if it had anything to do with her, she needed to know.

If Andrew wasn't her friend, that was fine; she was okay to walk away from him. But putting him in the enemy category? Well, that was a whole lot harder. After what she had just seen though, she realized that she would have to consider the issue. She heard a voice behind her. Turning, she saw Tallahassee off the leash, racing toward her.

Rhys called Tallahassee to heel, but it was too late.

Tallahassee sent her flying to the ground.

CHAPTER 7

TAYLOR CRIED OUT as her leg was jarred, while Tallahassee stood over her with a big sloppy grin on his face. She groaned as she stared up at him. "That kind of behavior will never be allowed." As she heard running footsteps, she turned to see Rhys racing toward her. She held up a hand. "I'm okay. You want to get this lug off me?"

"Instead I'll show you how." And, with a few simple commands, he had Tallahassee back off, sitting to her side, waiting for her to get up to her feet. Rhys gave her a hand to pull her up the rest of the way and said, "Sorry about that. He just got so excited when he saw you."

She looked down at the dog, who even now was inching to get closer. "You know what? In most cases, I'd have been pissed. But the fact that the dog is trying to get close to me? Well, maybe I'll forgive him after all."

Rhys laughed. "He shouldn't be jumping like that, and that's, indeed, a sign that his training has slipped, but we can work on that too."

"Sure," she agreed, with a nod.

"And, by the way, what were you doing?" She quickly explained. He frowned at her and asked, "You got that license plate?"

She nodded and told him, while he texted it to whoever he was working with.

"We'll figure out who that was pretty fast," he told her.

"And that just makes me feel guilty as shit," she admitted. "I don't want to be investigating my old friend."

"Maybe not," Rhys agreed, "but we do have to investigate whoever the hell has been shooting into your house. And while I was talking to Andrew's neighbors just now," he murmured, "I also got a call from a local detective. We have to go in and talk to him."

"And if I don't want to?" she asked, feeling everything inside of her shrink.

"If you don't want to, we don't," he stated. "But then this goes nowhere. If we don't cooperate with them, they won't cooperate with us."

"And the fact that they haven't cooperated yet?"

"Hey, this is a whole new detective, and this one comes with Badger's reference," Rhys explained. "So I'd give it a go, if I were you."

She groaned. "Fine, but I want to take Tallahassee with me."

"Good idea. By the way, I'm coming too."

She nodded. "Good thing. I don't think I'd make it on my own if you didn't."

He smiled. "You'll be just fine. I promise. Both of us will come and be support animals."

She snorted. "You don't look anything like a support animal."

"What?" he asked, giving her an injured look. "Of course I do. I'm very supportive."

"Sure, … maybe if something's in it for you."

He shot her a surprised look.

She shrugged. "That's probably not fair, but it kind of fits the mood I'm in."

"We'll have to change that," he said, "because I can't have you going in to the cops all aggressive. That'll just get their backs up, and shit'll hit the fan."

She groaned. "Now you tell me."

RHYS KNEW TAYLOR wasn't at all happy about today, between Andrew's disbelief and this new detective to test out, but Rhys wasn't happy that she hadn't stayed in the vehicle either. Still, they had to work together in order to sort out this mess. And first off was the detective. As he drove toward the police station, he looked over at her. "Is there anybody here who has worked with you in a good way?"

She shrugged and shook her head. "I don't really know anybody here now. Most of my bad memories of the cops are from my childhood."

"And from the break-in?" She nodded. "Let's see what this guy's got to say for himself."

"And do we trust him?"

"If he comes recommended from Jager and Badger, then yes," Rhys noted, "but nobody can ever really know what anybody is like until the situation is upon us."

"Right, so I'm not even sure what the point is of talking to him."

"The point is, we have a shooter after you," he reminded her. "And that's nothing to fool around with."

"Sure. I get that. I just don't know why we have to even involve them anymore."

"You think you can handle it yourself?" he asked, looking over at her.

"No, probably not," she admitted, "but that doesn't mean they'll help either."

"Why don't we stave off the judgment on that, and we'll go talk to him and see?"

She was quiet for the rest of the trip, and he couldn't blame her. She was mixed-up, confused, probably blindsided by Andrew's disbelief. She expected to have absolutely zero results from the local cops because of what had happened to her in her childhood and so far in the military too. With nobody being there to help her out on Colby's sexual harassment and now with this drive-by shooting issue, she distrusted authority, and that was a bigger problem. He pulled up at the police station, hopped out, and watched as she got Tallahassee out, smiled as she became a little more comfortable with each step. She was still rickety on her legs but refusing to let it drop her.

"You're doing really well on the leg," he mentioned, as she came around the corner of the truck.

"Meaning, I haven't wiped out in front of you yet," she quipped, then flashed him a grin. "But the day is young."

He burst out laughing. "The day is, indeed, young, but let's hope that you make it all the way through without a hitch."

"Did you fall?" she asked, halfway to the police station sidewalk.

He nodded. "Many times. I mean, I was so thrilled to get back on both legs, but, well, it wasn't easy, and that was with just one problematic leg. A buddy of mine lost both, and he did incredibly well, but I was there helping him get back up on his feet, and then I'd end up wiping out too." Rhys smiled in remembrance. "So maybe my memories are better than yours, at least in that aspect."

"I didn't really have anybody to help me up or down," she noted.

He didn't say anything for a long moment. "I know you don't think you've come very far, and you have a long way to go, but I see somebody who's gotten over the worst of it. This is the adaptation part. Every day you'll see progress. Every day you'll see something improving. I get it. It's hard. It's frustrating, and you want it to go way faster. Yet you have come so far that you need to stop and to remind yourself about the journey and not just the end."

She nodded. "You're not the first to tell me that."

"Of course not. Unfortunately, when we're in therapy, dealing with all the crap that goes down in our life, everybody's pretty free with advice, aren't they?"

She gave him a sharp look and then laughed. "You too, *huh?*"

"Oh, yeah," he confirmed, with a groan. "How I should be grateful, how I should be thankful, how I should be waking up every morning and, you know, praise the Lord that I'm alive. Yeah, I get it. But also plenty of days you wake up and you think, *I don't want to be alive. I can't do this anymore*," he shared. "And yet, you know, no matter when you go to bed, you still wake up the next day, and you gotta do it again."

"Whether you like it or not," she agreed, with a nod. "And sometimes it just feels like it's a *not*."

"Of course it is," he noted. "Sometimes things in life are a bigger challenge than we're really prepared for. It's not that it's bigger than us. It just *feels* like it's bigger than us."

She didn't say anything, as they walked into the station. Rhys walked up to the desk and identified himself and said they were there to meet Detective Django. The woman just nodded and told him to take a seat. As soon as they sat down, their names were called. Rhys looked over to see a man standing in front of an open inner door, frowning at them. Rhys frowned right back, but he stood, gave Taylor a hand up, and said, "This is us."

And, with that, the two of them—and Tallahassee—walked to the detective's office.

He studied the dog at their side and stated, "We shouldn't have him in here."

"Good," Taylor replied, her tone on the bitter side. "Let's go outside and talk."

His eyebrows shot up. He looked over at Rhys. "Well, let's make an exception in this moment. I'm not even exactly sure what I can do to help you."

"I'm not sure there's anything you can do either," she stated blithely, as she walked ahead, keeping Tallahassee at her side.

So much for Taylor not coming on aggressively with the local authority. "And yet," Rhys was quick to say, "if we don't tell you, then it'll be a problem."

"What's this about a shooting of some kind?" he asked, looking over him. "Why didn't you call the cops?"

"We did, and I guess they probably did something, but I don't really know what they did." She looked back at Rhys.

He shrugged. "I contacted Jager instead of the cops. Who contacted you?"

"Jager," he confirmed, with a nod. "And I've never had any reason not to trust him before."

"No, neither have I," Rhys stated. "So why don't we just go on the presumption that neither Taylor nor I are nuts, and we're here because there's a problem."

"Good enough," Django said. At his office he motioned

for them to take a seat. Tallahassee, with a complete lack of grace, collapsed onto the floor, like he hadn't had a good nap in months. The detective looked down at him and grinned. "Looks like quite a character." He frowned at Rhys. "Something about a War Dog?"

Rhys nodded and gave him a short explanation of how Rhys came to be here.

Django turned to Taylor. "And you ended up with him. Lucky you."

"Maybe," she said cautiously. "I mean, we've certainly hit it off. I've not got the experience that Tallahassee might need."

"I'm not sure about that," the detective disagreed. "I think a lot of the times dogs just need a firm hand, some guidance, and love. Maybe you have those things in spades."

"Absolutely," she noted. "I also could use a watchdog."

"And that brings us to why you're here," Django said. "Now you want to start from the beginning?"

"How far back do you want me to go?" she asked curiously.

His eyebrows shot up. "How far back is there?"

"Quite a bit," she murmured.

"How about the truncated version then."

And that's what she gave him, his gaze going to Rhys several times during her monologue. When she ran out, he asked Rhys, "And is this the story as far as you know it?"

"Yes, we did speak with Andrew earlier today. He said that he didn't know anybody, didn't know anything about this, and that he couldn't have imagined that his *best friend* Colby would do this. But I went around to the back of his house right after we left him, and he was talking on the phone. Then somebody drove up, who he seemed to argue with, yet he got in the vehicle and then took off with whomever."

"And you think it was Colby?" the detective asked Rhys.

"No, I don't know for sure it was him. I'm not saying that. For all I know this guy is someone else in town, and Colby hired somebody to torment her."

"Sounds like a real dick move."

"It *is* a real dick move," Rhys agreed, "but we also know that that doesn't mean it's not him."

"No, we absolutely don't know it's him." Django shook his head. "It would be really shitty if that is what's going on."

"Indeed, it would," Rhys murmured. And he fell silent, staring at the detective.

"Can't really do much about the military side of this," Django explained. "A shooter into your house? That's a whole different story though." He frowned at that. "I'll send over a team to investigate. However, from what you've told me, Rhys, you found no slugs in the house itself. We'll still take a look at it. I don't suppose you have anything else to corroborate this?"

"Yes, Jager sent me the information on the license plate of the truck, and apparently it was stolen."

Django wrote that down. "Jager didn't mention any of this to me."

"No, he was probably leaving it to me to explain," Rhys said.

"Okay, I need those details then."

He quickly gave him the information on the truck that had done the shooting and the information he had from Jager and the license plate number she'd just seen from the vehicle that had picked Andrew up.

"I'll double-check with Jager on this," Django shared,

"to make sure that we're clear."

"What you mean is, you'll double-check to make sure that we're not idiots," she stated.

Django looked at her, startled, and shrugged. "Jager's the one who called me. You didn't. I would like very much to confirm all these events before we go too deep into this."

"Honestly I'm not expecting you to do anything. I thought it was a waste of time to even come."

He looked at her in surprise. "You don't have much faith in law enforcement, I gather."

She snorted. "You'll find that most people here don't have much faith in anything I say." She added, "I'm part of the Moore family, and believe me. They had a bad rap for a very long time here."

"Well, I've not been here very long," Django said, "and I'm certainly not hindered by those kinds of prejudices. Maybe you should tell me just what that means here."

She shrugged. "My parents got into an awful lot of arguments. A ton of domestic violence calls were made from my mom." With all the information transferred over, she looked over Rhys. "I need to go home and lie down."

He nodded. "It's been a busy morning," he agreed, "not to mention you've been on the leg too much."

She shrugged. "I'll have to get used to it someday."

"I gather it's a recent amputation," Django said.

"Yes," she said, "or at least, recent on a prosthetic." Using the desk she stood and called Tallahassee toward her. He immediately bounded to his feet and stepped up to her side. She reached a hand down, gently stroked his fur. "He really is a good boy."

"Yes, he is," the detective agreed. "And he seems to care."

"I think he's had a tough few months, and, if this is some sort of homecoming for him, I don't think he'll argue," she murmured.

"No, I don't think so either." He smiled at them. "I'll get back to you with information on this." He looked over at Rhys. "And I'll contact Jager."

"Go ahead. I've been in contact with him and Badger already today."

"Badger's one of his partners, isn't he?"

"Yes, Jager I know personally, but Badger's the same ilk."

Django nodded. He walked them back outside, stopped, and watched as Taylor and Tallahassee got into the vehicle. "It is a scary thought to think that somebody is trying to shoot at her," he told Rhys.

"More than that," Rhys stated, "I think it's also part of the same military issue. We also don't know if it's an active investigation in the military."

Django nodded. "I'm not sure that anybody'll tell me that information either."

"I can get that information," Rhys stated, "or at least Badger can."

"Good enough," Django said, "then I'll catch up with you tomorrow." And, with that, he headed back inside.

Once Rhys joined her in the truck, she asked, "What was that all about?"

"He was just wondering how to find out information on whether the military case is active or not."

She shrugged. "They'll tell you it's active but won't do anything about it."

And he knew where she was coming from because, well, so much bureaucracy was the same thing. They told you one thing, but they were really just not ready to tell you anything important. And then later they would come along and dash your hopes, after you had been thinking something would move, and instead it didn't. "Let's stay the course," he murmured.

She shrugged. "It's not like I have any choice."

As they got back into the truck, he asked, "How's the leg?"

"It sucks," she murmured, "but I'll make it. Why? What do you want to do?"

"Nothing. We do need to go home, but do you have dog food and all the necessities for Tallahassee?"

"I do, but I don't really have much in the way of leashes, just what I grabbed from the pet store."

"And it's not great, but I can go there later today and pick up a few extras."

She shrugged. "If you feel like it, I'm not too bothered."

And he could tell from the lack of strength to her voice that she was backing off because of pain. He drove her home, and, as soon as he got her inside, he said, "I'll leave you with Tallahassee, and then I'll head out and do a little bit of reconnaissance around town." At that, she turned to join him, and he shook his head. "Nope, I want you to stay here."

"Are you going back over to Andrew's place?"

"I'll probably hit it on my way, just to see if there's any activity," he replied. "However, I'm more concerned about the previous known address for your buddy Colby, his family, anybody who might be interested in seeing him."

"You mean, you won't leave it to the local cops?" she asked, with half a smile, as if already knowing his answer.

"Nope, wasn't thinking to anyway."

"Good. Can't say I have a whole lot of faith in them anymore."

"You never did," he noted, "not from your childhood. I gather they didn't come once or twice?"

"Yeah, you could say that. My parents ended up basically getting blacklisted because the calls were just too often on their part. And I get that. I really do, but, as a child, it was hard to see it continue and to not have anybody step up and help. When it got really bad, I would call because I was petrified. Yet you can bet that they were damn slow to come."

"But they did come?"

"They came, but not until my mother broke my father's nose, and my father had broken her arm."

He just stared wordlessly at her.

She nodded. "Yeah, that was my childhood. So, if you drink, don't drink around me. I won't tolerate it. And I don't get drunk either, however I will occasionally enjoy a few drinks but never to excess."

"Not at all," he said. "I enjoy the occasional beer, but that's it."

"If the occasional beer doesn't turn you into a raving lunatic, we're fine," she stated. "My parents? Well, they were not fine."

With that, he gave her a gentle smile and said, "I promise." And he quickly turned and left.

Tallahassee barked at the front door, as Rhys walked away. He turned back and said, "You stay here, Tallahassee. I'll be back in a little bit. Stand guard."

CHAPTER 8

TAYLOR COULD TELL that Tallahassee didn't like Rhys driving away in the truck solo, but Tallahassee slowly returned to her side, collapsed to the floor, and gave her a woeful look. She smiled, reaching down a hand to pat him. "It would always just be us anyway, buddy," she murmured. "Get used to it. Either that or you need to go with him, if you won't be happy here."

The dog just gave her a tail wag, curled up on the floor beside her, and fell asleep.

She wasn't even sure what to do with that, but at least it was some kind of an answer. Now all she could do was rest and wish that her post-surgical recovery had gone beyond this point, so that she wasn't quite so helpless—although that wasn't a word she would ever have used to describe herself. The fact of the matter was, right now she couldn't do a whole lot compared to what she used to do or what she wanted to do. Right now she could handle only just so much. And, with a note of exhaustion, she curled up on the couch and fell asleep.

When she woke again, the sun's position already told her that it was afternoon, possibly late afternoon. She stared at the lowered sun before attempting to move because it would be painful. Anytime she got up after a long rest, it was beyond painful. But she didn't have a whole lot of choice.

She made her way back up to vertical, and, with a start, she sensed no sign of Tallahassee or of Rhys. She straightened and walked over to the living room window and looked outside. Rhys's rental truck wasn't back. She let out a whistle, but it was hoarse and not her normal range. She tried again, and, with that, she heard a bark. She turned and followed the noise to the rear of the house, finding Tallahassee outside in the backyard.

"How the hell did you get out here?" she asked and opened the back door for him. He bounded in and sniffed her all over, as if she had been gone. "I'm not the idiot that got out."

A frisson of fear slid down her back, as she realized that somehow that door had been opened. Was it possible that Rhys had opened it? And left it open? She didn't think so. But maybe he'd come back and had seen her sleeping and had decided to leave her asleep, while letting Tallahassee out. That would be the last time she took painkillers in the afternoon. She's slept for four hours.

Shaking her head, she quickly made a trip to the bathroom and then to the kitchen and put on coffee. She wished Rhys was back already, but four hours itself wasn't such a long time. Now if only he would come home and tell her that he had left the door open.

With the coffee on, she stepped into the fenced-in backyard and looked around. She found no sign of anything untoward and certainly nothing that would cause the dog to want to be out here—at least she didn't think so. But sleeping aided by her pain pills had knocked her out pretty heavily. So, for all she knew, somebody had come in through her backyard into her kitchen, and she would never have known. And that made her feel even more insecure.

Frowning, she did a full walk-through of the house with the dog at her side, trying to make sure that everything was okay. She didn't see anything wrong, and, when she returned to the kitchen to pour herself a cup of coffee, she stepped outside again onto the back porch and looked around.

And there, beside her, was a bullet, just sitting on the back porch.

She looked at it, hating the fear that it immediately engendered. She didn't know why somebody would do that, but it had to be related to the drive-by shooting. Maybe they'd decided that that was no longer a good thing to repeat, after the cops had been brought in, plus with Rhys here. If nothing else, maybe Rhys's presence would deter somebody from getting to be quite so bold. Yet this was bold enough. And a stranger in the backyard should be enough to cause Tallahassee to likely go out on his own.

But then why the hell wasn't a downed body out here? She almost laughed at that and then groaned because it wasn't very funny. If somebody needed to be taken down, would Tallahassee do that? Or would he worry and wait for a command? She had no idea and also had no idea how much danger she could possibly be in.

She took her coffee and wandered the back porch, considering just what she was supposed to do now. All of this was too much and brought more upset in her world. When her phone buzzed, she looked down to see a message from Rhys. It startled her for a moment before she remembered they'd exchanged contact numbers earlier.

At the grocery store, picking up groceries. What do you need?

She stared at the message, so mundane and so opposite to all the things going through her mind. She didn't even quite know how to answer. Finally she texted him back. **Dinner.** And remembering that she was low on coffee, she added that too. **Coffee.**

He gave her a thumbs-up, and that was it. She wasn't even sure what to do with that. But obviously something was going on here, and he was part of it. He didn't seem to make any effort to want to leave, and, right now, she could really use the houseguest. It would only delay the inevitable of being alone and trying to deal with life in her new world, but she'd take all of that delay that she possibly could.

She took a picture of the bullet and quickly sent it to Rhys.

When he called seconds later, he asked, "What the hell is that?" His tone was harsh.

"I found it on the back porch," she replied, proud that her voice was only a little shaky.

"Did you see who dropped it there?"

"I had a nap after you left." She hesitated and added, "Honestly I just woke up. And then fortunately whoever was here is long gone."

"And Tallahassee?"

"That's another part that I don't understand," she explained. "I thought the back door was locked. Did you open it? All I know is Tallahassee was outside, in the backyard, when I woke up."

"I'm on my way home," he said, his voice hard. "Go back inside with Tallahassee and close and lock the doors."

"You think it's something major?" she asked.

First came silence on the other end. And then he added, "Do you really think it can be anything else?"

"I think somebody's yanking my chain again," she replied bitterly. "I didn't tell you that some things were written in my file about me being mentally disturbed."

He hesitated. "We'll talk about that file, as soon as I get home. I also want to know who would have access to it."

"I have no idea," she admitted. "I guess you didn't get to that page, did you?"

"Nope, I guess I didn't," he muttered, and his voice was distracted. "Like I said, get in the house, and I'll be there in fifteen."

Not sure that she needed to, but she walked into the house with Tallahassee, locked the back door then headed right through to the living room, where she could watch for Rhys to return. As she sat down and waited for Rhys, she wondered at how her life had suddenly flipped. Not only was Rhys in it but so was Tallahassee. The War Dog seemed to understand that she was upset and immediately sat at her feet and dropped his chin on her knees.

She smiled at him. "You're such a pretty boy," she murmured. His tail wagged, but a whine came from the back of his throat. She nodded. "I know. I don't know what's going on. I don't know why. I don't know how," she stated. "I just know that something really shitty is going down in Dodge. And we do not want any part of it."

But getting out of this would not be the same thing. As she looked out the window from the back of the couch, she saw a car drive past her house suspiciously slow. She strained her eyes to figure out who it was, but the vehicle was too far away for her to see such details, like who the driver was. Yet she noted he wore a baseball cap pulled down low.

Suspicious as hell, she stepped out on the front porch and tried to read the license plate. The vehicle, seeing her, took off. Fast. At that, Tallahassee was much more interested now in the goings-on around her, stepped forward, and started to bark. She looked around to see what he was barking at, but he was staring down the road at the vehicle that was now long gone.

"I don't know," she muttered to the space around them. "Seems to me like your reaction time's a little bit on the slow side."

He just looked at her, and his tail wagged.

At least the driver had seen that she had a dog. But then whoever dropped off the bullet on her rear porch had seen the dog too. As she stepped forward to go back inside, she noticed a neighbor standing out and watching. Taylor raised a tentative hand, and the older woman just looked at her. Obviously not too interested in being friendly, the neighbor lady stepped back into her house and slammed the door shut.

"*Great*. Not exactly the best way to get to know the neighbors."

When she heard another vehicle roar up, she stepped back inside the front door. Sure enough, this time it was Rhys. He pulled into the driveway, hopped out with the groceries, and saw her standing there.

He frowned. "That's hardly locked inside and resting."

"Maybe not, but some guy was driving past really slow," she murmured. "I wanted to see if I could get his license plate."

He stopped and stared and looked around. "How long ago?"

"A couple minutes or more. He's gone," she relayed, with a shrug. "I did get a picture of the vehicle but not the license plate."

"Let me see it," he said. She pulled it up on her phone, and he nodded. "That at least is something. Maybe not enough to do anything with, but the trouble is, I don't know if he was just curious. Maybe he's looking to buy property in this neighborhood."

"I don't ... I don't know," she murmured.

"We'll just keep an eye out for him," he noted. "Absolutely no way to know at this point in time." He handed her a bag of groceries and said, "I'll go get the rest."

She took them into the kitchen and started putting them away and realized he'd bought steaks. Such a male food choice. She said as much to him, when he came in with the second bag.

"Well, you said get dinner, but you didn't say what, so I grabbed what I would normally eat," he explained. "What's the matter? You don't like steak?"

"I love steak," she replied, "but I don't have a barbecue." He stopped and stared. "At least a barbecue pit is out there. I just ... I don't know if it works or not."

"That'll be the first thing I check," he stated, with a headshake, as he disappeared outside.

She smiled as the two males disappeared outside to inspect the big barbecue. It had been here when she moved in, and she'd never bothered to do anything with it. Neither had her parents before her. She probably should, but she could only handle so much at one time, and that just didn't make the cut.

When Rhys came back in again, he smiled. "It works just fine. It needs a good cleaning. I'll work on that next. Steaks deserve to be barbecued."

She smiled. "If you say so."

He mock-glared at her. "Are you making fun of me?" he asked in a suspiciously light tone.

She shrugged. "Hey, it's better than breaking down."

"Yeah, don't do that," he replied.

She laughed. "No, I won't. It's been a long time since I've let myself do it."

"Maybe you should then. Sometimes you just need the release."

"Maybe," she agreed. "Release can happen other ways too." At that, he stopped and looked at her, one eyebrow raised. She flushed, shook her head. "No, I didn't mean it that way."

He waggled his eyebrows. "Well, anytime you do mean it that way ..."

But his expression was so comical that the only thing she could do was laugh. And, with that laughter, she felt tears trying hard to escape. She shook her head. "As much as I want to laugh, I'm afraid it will quickly turn into something else."

"Got it," he noted. "In that case, you work on a salad and some starch to go with those steaks. I picked up baby potatoes. If you're okay with that, I'll throw them on the barbie instead."

"Is that possible?" she asked.

"Absolutely." He stared at her, frowning. "I guess you haven't barbecued much."

"No, haven't at all," she admitted, "but I'm willing to take your lead on this."

He grinned. "Be willing to take my lead on all kinds of things if you want." And, with that last comment, he disappeared out the back.

It's a good thing he left because she was just flustered enough not to know what to say to him. And yet it had all been done in good fun, and there was no pressure; at least she didn't feel any pressure.

She didn't want there to be any pressure. He was a nice guy, and she wanted things to stay pressure-free. She didn't even know what that meant though. She was such an idiot; she was just the kind of person who would walk into a situation completely blind and not realize that somebody was chatting her up.

The guys in the forces, even the gals, used to laugh at Taylor and say that she was deliberately being obtuse. Yet she wasn't; she just didn't recognize when sexual overtures were happening, even when directed right at her. Being more of a serious personality type, she wasn't the kind to do a whole lot of flirting. She'd gone into the army because she wanted to be of service. But she'd forgotten that people were the same everywhere.

And maybe that's what had gotten her into trouble with Colby. She didn't think so, and there'd never been anything between them, so why the hell would going into the army together matter? She didn't know. Yes, he'd also been higher up the food chain than she was, and maybe that illusion of power had changed him. She didn't know.

And, from then on, dinner passed as a more enviably and lighter affair.

When she sat back and rubbed her tummy, she said, "My gosh, that was good."

"See? It's all about the barbecuing."

She chuckled. "Now if only I had realized that barbecuing was so addictive."

"It definitely is," he murmured. "You just have to get used to it."

"Maybe. I'd have to learn how to use it."

"It's not hard," Rhys said. "I can teach you."

She looked at him, her eyebrows raised. "So apparently

you're volunteering to teach me all kinds of things. Just how long were you planning on staying close by?"

He laughed. "As long as I need to, apparently."

She shook her head. "I'm not sure it's that easy."

"It's never that easy," he replied, "but, at the moment, I'm pretty footloose, fancy-free."

"And you're okay with that?"

"For the moment, yes," he stated. "I definitely don't want to go back to my parents' house."

She laughed. "So you're running away from them."

"Maybe," he said, with a teasing glance. "Or maybe running to something better makes more sense."

She flushed. "You're such a flirt," she noted in amazement. "I never realized."

"I'm not normally either. I think it's something to do with you."

"Ha, that sounds like I'm getting the blame for something I didn't even know I was doing."

"No blame," he disagreed immediately. "Maybe credit."

She snorted at that. "Sounds once again like you're trying to make good on something."

"I am," he declared. "I like you. And you need help. So is there anything wrong with sticking around and helping?"

"No," she answered cautiously. "And, yes, I could use the help."

"Right. So, for the moment, I'm staying here. Good?" he asked her.

"Yes, fine." She wasn't exactly sure how she'd gotten into this roommate situation in the first place. "And you're right. I appreciate the help." She added, "I am doing much better with Tallahassee."

"Hey, Tallahassee just needed somebody to love him and

to be serious about looking after him. And that's worth a lot to me."

"He's a beautiful dog," she noted quietly. "I can't imagine what happened to him before now."

"I'm not sure either, and sometimes with these things we'll never know. The fact of the matter is, we have the dog now, and he's doing really well here, so I'm not too sure that he should be moved. As long as you're okay to look after him?"

"I'm okay," she replied. "I just am not exactly sure what his needs are or how to meet them."

"Maybe, but you're doing really well working on it," he said, with a beaming smile.

She looked at him and sighed. "You really are impossible sometimes."

"All the time, I hope," he teased. "Life's too short to buckle in and to hate your life. I went through that stage too."

"It's really weird knowing that you've been ahead of me in this whole scenario," she noted.

"Weird how?" he asked cautiously.

"I don't know. Just to know that somebody has gone through the same kind of pain and problems that I have," she explained, "somehow helps me adjust better. I had never really thought about other people on this journey."

"That's partly a good thing in the sense that my group in the VA center helped me," he said. "You may not have had that same experience, which I think would be sad because I think everybody deserves to have support in this world, and obviously you missed out on that."

"Obviously." She nodded. "I hadn't really realized that it was missing though."

"No, and we don't always," he agreed. "Until somebody like me comes along, and I can share about the good experiences that I had, which, to you, seems like a foreign … almost a foreign language."

"Yes," she agreed, "and yet I'm happy for you."

"Of course," he said. "You're not the kind to sit here and hate somebody because they had an easier time of it than you. You're somebody who would much rather get up and move on with it. The problem is, you got up and moved on with it when you weren't quite ready."

She glared at him. "Wow, you figured that out already, *huh*?"

"Absolutely." He grinned at her. "That's why you came home and had to take a painkiller today, when you really should be off the prosthetic entirely."

She winced. "Yeah, but then it's hard to get around."

"Sure, but you have crutches." He looked around and frowned. "I presume you have them somewhere."

"I do, and I hate them. I hate them with a passion."

He nodded. "You're not the first person to say that. And honestly I get it. I mean, they're not my favorite thing either."

"But you still expect me to get off this foot and use the crutches, right?"

"No, I don't expect you to do anything," he argued. "While I learned a lot at the VA center, I learned more practical stuff through Jager and his team. So I expect you to listen to your body and to do whatever you feel you need to do. I'm not the one to tell you what to do. I don't know your body. You have to figure it out yourself." She stared at him in shock. He shrugged. "Again, something that I learned at the center but better through Jager's team."

She just shook her head. "Obviously we went to very different centers."

He grinned. "Obviously. But I gotta tell you that I've never been happier than when I was there. I mean, it was an adjustment to leave and to move back into the real world, and it wasn't an easy adjustment, until I hooked up with Jager again," he noted. A few minutes later he asked, "So, agreed?"

"Agreed to what?" she asked, startled by his question.

"I guess I just feel better if I have your okay that I stick around."

"And here I thought I already gave it," she replied in a teasing voice.

"You did, but I don't want to overstay my welcome."

"No, I wouldn't want you to overstay your welcome either," she agreed, with a laugh. "So, yes, it's fine that you're staying for now. And we'll see how it goes. You've been a huge help already. And that is much appreciated." He nodded slowly. But she got the feeling he wasn't terribly impressed at her words. She didn't know what else to say, so opted out for an easy answer. "Why don't you take Tallahassee for a walk," she suggested, "and I'll do the dishes."

And, with that, she hopped up, gathered the dishes, and headed back to the kitchen.

RHYS WASN'T EXACTLY sure whether or not he'd pushed something too far or not; he had a tendency to. And he really did want to stick around. Yet he could have gone to a hotel. He frowned as he walked down the street with the dog, studying the neighbors. Was everybody unfriendly, or was it just her experience coloring everything? And he couldn't blame her if it was. Nothing like a bad scenario to taint your overview of the world around you. But, as he saw a couple neighbors outside, he waved, friendly-like. A couple waved back.

One guy stopped to talk to him about Tallahassee.

"That's quite the dog," he noted, with a bright smile.

"Indeed. He's a War Dog," Rhys explained, "now retired and gets to spend his days looking after Taylor here." And he pointed to her house.

"Good," the man agreed. "She's alone. Not a good scenario here."

"Is it a rough town?" he asked, curious.

"I wouldn't have said so, but a couple incidents over the last year made us realize that it's not quite the sweet town we had hoped it was."

"How long have you been here?" Rhys asked, hoping to get him to talk a little bit more.

"Not all that long," he replied cautiously. "I was raised in this town, so I was kind of hoping that coming back home again would have the same feel, but it doesn't. It's progress, but, like progress, not all of us are terribly happy to see it move on."

"And I get that," Rhys agreed, with a bright smile. "I know Taylor was raised here herself, but she's definitely struggling."

"Is she the one missing a leg?" he asked curiously.

At that, Rhys nodded. "Yes, she lost it in a military accident."

"Oh, poor woman," he said, with a headshake. "The town itself is, you know, pretty easy on you, but I haven't found it at all that easy to get to know people since I came back."

"I think she's having the same struggle," Rhys noted. "You want it to be easier than it is, but sometimes it just seems to take a little bit more out of you than you have to give. So then the next time you just don't give as much."

At that, the older man laughed. "Isn't that the truth?" he said appreciatively. "Anyway, tell her hi, and the next time she's out wandering around, she should stop and just visit for a bit. Now that I know who she is, I'm more than happy to visit."

"I'll tell her that," Rhys said, and he moved on.

He did that whenever he crossed paths with others, as he slowly wandered up and down the few blocks around her house—making social chitchat with some of the neighbors, just letting people know that Taylor was there and that she was not necessarily alone but that she had the War Dog with her. Some people were fascinated; some asked a lot of questions, and some seemed quite confused over what the whole thing meant.

"Does that mean the dog goes to war?" one woman asked, looking at Tallahassee and taking a step back.

"No, it means that he was a huge help in the war in which we still have multiple deployed troops," he noted. "And now the dog is retired and gets to come home and have a decent life."

"I'm really happy to hear that," she replied, as she understood a little better. "It's hard to imagine that these animals go to the fighting."

"Most of the time they're bomb trained to sniff out buried mines. But we have all kinds of training that goes into different aspects of that for them."

"And you?" she asked. "Are you staying with her?"

"I am for a while," he noted.

"And that's good," she agreed. "I used to know the family." And she frowned. "All three generations. The middle one was the worst."

"Taylor told me something about her family and what a problem it was."

The woman looked at him with relief. "Such a problem. I mean the shouting and the screaming that used to go on all nights. We worried about the old lady but she left and moved somewhere else We couldn't help but worry about the girl. Lots of times we called the cops, and sometimes it seemed like they didn't really come. Or they came but they waited, as if to see if it would calm down before they got here. We couldn't really blame them, but, at the same time, it bothered me that the little girl was going through all that. I didn't want to see her taken away from her family and put into foster care, but sometimes you had to wonder if maybe that wasn't a better solution."

"She does mention it every once in a while," Rhys shared. "I imagine it was a pretty rough upbringing. I think it influenced her to join the military."

At that, the neighbor nodded. "You know what? I … I imagine it was her one way to get out. I don't know where her parents are now, and don't care, as long as they stay away. It's been peaceful since they moved out."

"And that's good," he agreed.

He called Tallahassee to him, waved goodbye, and kept on walking. He was checking out the neighbors and also trying to see how people viewed Taylor, now that she was back again. Taylor hadn't had it easy growing up, and, if the people found it hard to forget, that would make it harder on her. At the same time, she shouldn't have to fight for some peace in her life.

He and Tallahassee slowly walked home to find a vehicle sitting on the opposite side of the street, across from her place. He frowned at that and whispered to Tallahassee, "I don't know, boy. What do you think?"

Tallahassee's hackles went up, as he assessed the vehicle.

"Yeah, that's my take too," Rhys agreed. "I don't like anything about this." He wandered closer, taking a photo of the back license plate. As the driver just appeared to be sitting there and doing nothing, Rhys approached and knocked on the driver's side window.

The guy was startled and rolled down the window.

Rhys smiled. "Hey, you got a problem? Can I help you with something?"

The guy looked at him and said, "Get lost."

Rhys's eyebrows shot up. "Wow, nice. And here I just thought maybe you're in trouble. I mean, you've been sitting here for a while."

"I have not," he snapped in disgust. "I'm waiting for somebody. Now get lost."

"*Tsk-tsk*," Rhys said, looking down at the dog. "I wouldn't upset my dog, if I were you."

"What the fuck do I give a shit about your dog for? Now get the hell out of here." He turned on the engine and asked, "What the hell's this neighborhood gone to?"

"Yeah, good question." Rhys studied the man. "Looks to me like you're casing the joint."

At that, the man's eyebrows rose. "You don't know fuck all."

"You might just be surprised at how much I do know," Rhys replied. "Don't suppose your name is Colby by any chance, is it?"

The other man's eyes widened, quick and fast. "Fuck off. You don't know me, and I don't know you."

"Maybe not. What I do know, I don't really like." And Rhys gave him a smile. "Raped any women lately?"

The stalker's face turned ashen. "Don't you even start talking like that. That's just complete bullshit. Besides I'm not Colby." And, with that, he hit the gas pedal and took off.

CHAPTER 9

TAYLOR STEPPED ONTO the front porch and asked, as Rhys approached, "Who was that?"

He shook his head. "I don't know, but it was somebody who didn't like being questioned."

"Did you get a license plate?"

He nodded, as he worked on texting the license plate info to the detective.

"Can we report people for sitting out there?" she asked. "That seems kind of mean."

He looked over at her and shook his head. "Nothing mean about this now. Shooting into your house is a whole different level of shithead."

"I get that, but I didn't recognize him."

"And he said his name wasn't Colby."

"No, it wasn't Colby, but ..." Then she frowned and paused. "He does have this frat-like buddy system with a couple guys. At least they were always the other ones he visited with when we were in town," she murmured. "But that kind of looked like Joland, Colby's brother. He was part of the same group. I just haven't seen him in probably ten, maybe even twelve years, so I couldn't be sure."

"And yet, if he's doing something for his brother, chances are his ride was another stolen vehicle." At that, his phone rang. He stepped inside, motioning at her to come in with

him. "Yeah," he answered. "Did you get a rundown on it? …
Stolen. Really? Okay, so that just puts it into the same
category as our shooter," he murmured. "She thought it was
Colby's brother, his first name is Joland, but couldn't be sure
it was him. Could have been just a friend of Colby's,
somebody he used to visit with all the time, a kind of frat-
buddy scenario. Yeah, I don't know names."

He looked over at her with a raised eyebrow. She shook
her head. "No, she doesn't know either." He listened to the
detective on the other end of the call, then asked her, "How
would we find out?"

"I don't know." And then she stopped and added, "Andrew would know."

"Oh, good," Rhys said, "another reason to go visit him."
And he gave her a wolfish look.

"You can't touch him," she declared.

In the background she heard the detective speaking.
"Hey, whoa, whoa, whoa, whoa. What do you mean, touch
him?"

"Nothing," Rhys said, with a hard tone, "but I know
somebody who apparently does know who this guy might be.
I didn't get a picture of his face, but, if I can get a last name
and a mug shot, I can confirm whether it was him or not."

Taylor interrupted, "Maybe the detective should go
check this out."

"Chances are you're so damn busy that you won't bother," he told Django in a tart tone. "I can make a quick trip
and knock on Andrew's door. If he answers, I'll let you
know. If he doesn't, then it's all good."

"No, it's not all good," the detective said. "I'll go.
What's this guy's address?"

Rhys gave him the address, and the call ended.

"I'll go anyway," Rhys said to Taylor.

"No, no." Taylor shook her head. "That's not a good idea."

"It *is* a good idea," he argued. "One, I need to find out if this detective will do what he says he'll do, and, two, if he goes to the front door, and this Andrew asshole sneaks out the back, like he did before, we want to make sure that we have a talk with him."

She hesitated, and then her shoulders sagged. "Fine, but I'm coming too."

He immediately shook his head. "No, you're too sore."

She glared at him. "Like hell. It's not up to you to tell me that I'm too sore to do anything."

He grinned at her. "Absolutely it's not up to me." He chuckled. "And I do like it when you get feisty."

She flushed again and murmured, "There you go, teasing again."

"Hey, I'll be happy to take it past teasing," he offered, "anytime you're ready."

"I'm not ready," she stated.

"I know," he said gently. "I get that, and I won't push." She glared at him. He smiled. "See? I'll be good."

"You don't know how to be good," she said in a rough tone.

He shook his head. "You're wrong there. I do know, and I also know that this is just teasing to ease the seriousness of what's going on here," he stated. "I would never push anything. Particularly after knowing what you went through."

"Colby didn't rape me," she repeated. "And, I think, in a way, because I did fight him off, that's why the military police were less concerned about it, and, yet, at the same time, I think it's also what aggravated Colby."

"Well, that's just shit. So you get punished for being smart enough to have self-defense skills that can keep you safe?" He shook his head at that. "That's just wrong on all levels."

She smiled. "I forgot you were such a champion of lost causes," she noted in a light tone. But inside she was delighted that he'd accepted her word for it. "Besides, you know that a lot of these guys, they just, … well, it makes them angry when you do succeed."

"Absolutely. Most of these guys are angered or challenged to do something about it when you do succeed," he noted. "Another reason for you to stay here, instead of coming with me on this trip."

And realizing she'd walked into that trap, she immediately shook her head. "Oh no you don't," she snapped. "I don't want to sit here as the *good little woman* and wait for you to come home, after solving my problems."

He stared at her. "That never even occurred to me," he said. "All I was trying to do was preserve the swelling on your leg."

She flushed as she looked down. "How do you know it's swollen?"

"Because every time you take a step, you're wincing," he stated. "Your leg is not doing well, and you're stubborn enough to keep at this, even though you've been given an out to relax it."

"I'll come and stay in the vehicle," she suggested.

He stared at her for a long moment. "Okay, that's a compromise I can live with."

She was surprised and asked, "Seriously?"

"Yes, of course." He frowned. "Isn't compromise in your

portfolio?"

"Sure, I just didn't think it was in yours."

And, with that smart retort, she walked out the front door, Tallahassee on a leash. Even as they walked to his truck, Tallahassee gave a bark. Rhys looked at the War Dog and smiled. "You're getting quite comfortable here, aren't you, bud?"

Tallahassee wagged and greeted him all over again.

"Does he always greet you like he hasn't seen you in forever?" she asked, as they got into the vehicle.

"Lots of dogs do that," he noted. "It's a sense of starting to understand who's family and who's not."

"Except, when you leave, it'll be hard on Tallahassee," she said.

Rhys thought about it and nodded. "And equally hard on me. That was part of the reason why I didn't want to keep training animals. I wanted to have deeper, longer-term relationships with some of them, and it broke me down to lose them—either to a transfer to another handler or in death on the field. Most of the guys didn't really get it either. Although a lot of us struggled with the losses."

"I can't imagine," she stated. "Surely there's a lot of good to keeping the relationships real like that."

"There is," he said, "absolutely there is, but they're working dogs, and they have jobs to do, and that doesn't necessarily include being that person who gets to be with them all the time. They had handlers. They had trainers. Dogs moved around a lot. Sometimes they were in one division, and they stayed there, but, if they had an aptitude for something else, they would get moved just as easily."

"And you didn't get moved with them?"

"A lot of times the trainers, handlers, did not get moved

with the War Dogs," he noted. "And you know? For a lot of people, that was totally okay. To them, the dog was a tool."

She winced at that. "God, I can't imagine ever thinking of a dog like this as a tool. He feels like family."

"And that's how a dog is supposed to feel, how a pet is supposed to feel," Rhys agreed. "There's no room for that kind of sentiment in the military though."

"There should be," she stated. "How can it be wrong to care about your animals?"

"It isn't, but don't forget, in the military, they aren't considered animals. They're assets."

She shook her head as he drove down to Andrew's place again. "Do you really think Andrew has something to do with this?"

"I'll just say that his behavior this morning was suspicious."

"I know it was, but maybe he has a reasonable explanation."

"I hope so. I really do because otherwise he's just looking like a bigger shit every time I see him."

She snorted at that. "I didn't have a whole lot to say to him when he quit the service, but he was pretty angry at me for not quitting with him. He felt like we'd deceived him apparently. Like made it into being some sort of romantic step forward in our lives, you know? Like working for our country and all the rest, but he didn't take to it the way Colby and I did."

"You were looking for an easy out from the life that you were stuck in," he noted, "whereas this Andrew guy probably had completely different plans or a completely different childhood and wasn't looking with the same desperation."

She slid him a sideways glance. "You figured that out

too, *huh*? You're kind of dangerous."

"No," he disagreed. "Once you understand what someone's childhood is like, you see it all over again. We have a lot of people who went into the service, for one reason or another, into one division or another, because they needed to get away. So, once they were old enough, they were gone. And, as you know, it's pretty hard to argue with anybody who's unhappy enough that that seems like their best answer."

"And yet I'm sure that's why a lot of people enlisted."

"It's how tons of people enlisted," he agreed. "But is that the right way? I don't know. It suits some people. It does not suit others. That's why you do your tour, and you're in or out."

She smiled. "Exactly, and I should have gotten out before I got blown up."

"Maybe," he said, "but that's only due to hindsight. You couldn't foretell the future."

"Something that I never did get very good at," she murmured.

"Does anybody? I mean, I got injured myself, and, if I were capable, I would still be there. But I didn't want a desk job, and I don't want anything different than the life that I had with the navy," he shared. "So now I'm trying to find a new life."

"And that's the reality of living for everybody, isn't it?" she said. "You do what you can, and, when you can't do it anymore, for whatever reason—burnout, fired, blown up— you move on."

He smiled. "I like what you said there too because it's very real. I mean, we do what we can, but, when we can't do the same thing anymore, there just isn't the same space for us. Whether we like it or not, it's up to us to create a new reality and to find a new life. And I'm still looking for mine."

"And you have time," she noted.

"Well, it depends." He grinned at her. "I might be an uninvited house guest for a while."

She snorted at that. "As long as you buy groceries and can barbecue, you pretty well are a shoo-in at your current place."

He chuckled. "Well, I'm working on the owner. She's got this great sense of humor, and she's really sexy, but she's got a bit of a chip on her shoulder and thinks that, you know, life's just too tough sometimes."

She stared at him. "Wow, all of that too, *huh?*" But it was hard for her to even talk. He thought she was sexy? "Besides, you need to get your eyes checked," she muttered.

He looked at her in surprise. "Why is that?"

"I don't think in any way that I'm sexy anymore," she stated, with a headshake.

"Ah, that's because you're thinking only of your missing leg," he noted, with a smile. "Remember? I've got one of those issues too."

"Yeah, but somehow I can't see you thinking that you aren't sexy anymore."

He smiled. "I think we all go through a stage of *Will anybody want us? Will anybody give a shit, or am I just too ugly now?* The fact of the matter is, we all have days like that."

"Even you?" she challenged.

"Even me," he confirmed, with a smile. "Just not for very long."

"Do you really think Andrew's involved?"

"He's involved in something," Rhys stated quietly. "What I don't know is whether he's involved in this or not. I couldn't get a read on him while we were there the first time," he admitted. "I'm usually pretty good at it too."

"He's different too, since he got out of the army," she noted. "He didn't use to be like this. And I know there's a certain amount of anger over what he would consider was the system in the army."

"Ah, well, there's certainly enough guys who come out of the military angry too." Rhys shrugged. "To each his own. Everybody has to make their own decisions."

"I guess my questions is, do you think he's doing something actively to help Colby?"

"I don't have an answer for that. It would be nice if we did, but we don't, not yet," he said. "We will get them though."

"I wonder," she murmured.

He gave her a one-arm shrug. "Keep the faith. We're getting there now."

"No, we're not," she argued.

"Sure," he replied. "Whoever I caught watching your house just moments ago made a mistake. They were spying on your house, but they weren't aware of me."

"They didn't know about you," she corrected. "And the fact that you're even at my house, if it is Colby behind all this, just might make him even angrier."

"Meaning that you might have a partner now and somebody to help defend you?"

"I'm not even sure *defend* is the word that they would be concerned about. I think it would be more a case of he wouldn't want me to have a partner."

"So he's also the jealous type, is he?"

"I don't know why though," she said. "I never encouraged him."

"Unfortunately, that doesn't seem to matter with a lot of guys," he muttered. "Let's not worry about it for the moment. We'll figure out what's happening in that corner afterward. Right, now let's see if the detective even shows up. We need to know who we can trust and who we can't."

"And yet I thought a friend of yours recommended Django."

"He did, but I'd still like to double-check for myself."

She stayed quiet as they drove to Andrew's house again, after being here this morning. "It will not be nice for me, if Andrew's involved." She glanced at Rhys.

"And again, let's not go there yet," he said. "We will figure this out, but it'll take a little bit."

She just nodded and didn't say anything as they turned on the block where Andrew's house was.

"There is a vehicle outside his house," she said, pointing, while Rhys slowed down.

"There is. It's not the one we were looking for though."

"You mean, the same one parked outside my house earlier?" she asked. "Yet it is similar."

He studied it and nodded. "You're right there, but the detective should be here now." Then he watched as another man strode up the sidewalk and studied the address. He looked down at notes in his hand and walked forward. "That's Django."

"Well, that's good news," she said.

"At least he's following up," Rhys stated. "And depending on that other vehicle …"

"I know, but it's not the same license plate," Taylor said.

"That doesn't necessarily mean much," Rhys stated. "Our stalker slash spy could have just stolen another set and switched them out."

She turned and looked at him. "They can do that?"

"Piece of cake," he noted. "Especially for somebody who might be living on the edge of the law."

"Wow, I hadn't even considered that," she muttered. "But, I guess if you steal once, what's the difference?"

"Exactly." Rhys parked just before Andrew's house on the opposite side of the road, so they could watch as the detective approached Andrew's house.

She stared at Rhys. "What is it you're looking for?"

"Confirmation that this friend of yours is involved."

"I would just as soon not have that confirmation," she murmured.

He shot her a look. "I get that, but sticking your head in the sand never worked for me."

She smiled. "Gee, I can't imagine why."

He chuckled. "Keep up the good mood," he said. "So far nobody's answering the door, and yet somebody should be home."

"Just because a vehicle is parked out front, that doesn't mean anybody's home."

She frowned at that, but it made some kind of sense. And just as they thought nobody would answer, the door opened, and there was Andrew, pushing the hair out of his eyes.

"Looks like he was asleep again."

"I don't know if *sleep's* quite the right word, but he was occupied, and he's looking fairly stressed. And he probably doesn't know who this guy is either."

"No, I don't imagine he does."

At that, the detective showed him his ID and probably asked if he could come in. At least that's what she assumed he'd ask. Watching Andrew's body language, he wasn't being very cooperative. "What happens if Andrew doesn't let the detective in?"

"He can come back with a warrant and force an entry. He can do all kinds of stuff."

As Django turned and pointed to the car behind him, he asked several questions. Andrew just looked even more rattled, but he shrugged. They couldn't hear the conversation, which was kind of irritating too.

"Now if only we had a way to know exactly what was going on," she murmured.

"I know, but we'll do the best we can right now."

The detective stayed and talked with Andrew for a few more moments. And then he walked to the car and looked through the windshield to the dash. If stolen, with the wrong license plate on this vehicle too, the detective needed the VIN. And whether that was something that would pop up or not with a random search depended on the make and model.

Rhys turned on the engine and said, "Considering the detective showed up here, I presume that whoever drove that stolen vehicle to Andrew's went out the back."

She stared at Rhys in surprise. "Aren't you going out the back then to see?"

"I was," he stated, "but I won't leave you alone."

And now she realized the *real* reason he didn't want her to come.

RHYS LOOKED OVER, saw her expression, patted her hand, and said, "It's okay."

"No, it's not," Taylor argued. "I should have stayed home."

"And I understand why you didn't," he replied. "Sometimes we just have to do what we need to do. You needed to see this, so we're here."

She nodded. "But now I do feel foolish."

"Of course you do, but there's no need," he told her. "I'll drive around to the back and take a look and see if anybody's there. While the detective is still making inquiries, he's keeping Andrew busy. However, if our driver has any idea that they'll look at the vehicle, it shouldn't take too long to realize it's stolen. And, once that happens, this guy won't stick around."

"I wonder," she murmured. "I wonder if the detective will get the information he needs."

"Well, he showed up to do the job, which means he at least gets full marks in my book," Rhys noted. "Whether this friend of yours—"

"*Acquaintance*," she corrected him immediately. "I'm not sure that *friend* even counts anymore."

"Fine. If Andrew, this person you used to know, gives the detective the answers we need, that's a whole different story."

"Right," she said, with a headshake. "I can't even be sure that any of this is related to what happened to me."

"No, but we do know that somebody shot at your house," he reminded her. "Hang on to that thought. Everything else becomes secondary."

And, with that, she groaned. "I get it. I do, but it still sucks."

He nodded as he kept driving around the block. When he pulled in the back alley, he said, "Now, if they really are looking for the VIN on that vehicle, the guy inside is likely to either have already made his escape or is currently trying to make his escape." And, sure enough, as he studied the surrounding land, he pointed to a fence and asked, "Who's fence is that?"

"Looks like the neighbor's," she murmured.

"And there he is."

She smiled. "That looks like the same guy, the stalker slash spy guy who was watching my house."

"It absolutely is," Rhys confirmed. "Now I'll leave you alone."

She nodded. "Go," she said excitedly. "Go, go, go."

He snorted. "And I'm taking Tallahassee with me."

At that, Tallahassee barked and jumped up eagerly. "Yeah, you're always ready for some action, aren't you, buddy?"

He opened the door, got him out on a leash, and raced down so that he could catch up with this guy as he walked down the back street. The same back road that they had come past last time, where he'd seen Andrew with some guy in a truck. As Rhys raced toward this guy, the other guy turned and looked at him and frowned.

"What the hell?" he asked. "Are you following me?"

"No. I came to talk to Andrew," Rhys explained. "However, I know a detective talking to Andrew right now wants to have a talk with you."

At that, the guy said, "Shit." And he booked it as hard and as fast as he could.

At that, Rhys looked down at Tallahassee, knowing that his own prosthetic would give out against a two-legged male. So, giving the orders and the command, Rhys headed right after the dog, who ran for the man. Tallahassee quickly cornered him against a fence.

As he went growling closer, the other guy yelled, "I'll

fucking sue, and you go to jail for this. Nobody gets to have a dog like this around to hurt me."

"He hasn't hurt you yet," Rhys murmured. He called Tallahassee back ever-so-slightly. Tallahassee didn't like being ordered back though. With another command Tallahassee slowly stepped away, but he wasn't giving this guy any ground.

"Now," Rhys said, strolling toward his captive, "shall we talk about what you were doing parked outside Taylor's house?"

"I don't even know who you're fucking talking about," he yelled, as he glared at him.

"You know something? No need to speak to me. The detective wants to talk to you," he noted. "Pretty damn sure that vehicle you were sitting in was stolen."

"Was not," he said defensively. "I don't know anything about it."

"Well, you can tell your story to the detective," he said, as he pointed at the corner. And, sure enough, the detective stood there, glaring at them.

As Django walked closer, Tallahassee kept a nice low growl going to keep the prisoner in place. Rhys pointed to the guy. "This is the man who was parked outside of Taylor's house in that car now parked at Andrew's place."

"You don't know it was that car," the stalker guy said, with a sneer. "You didn't take a picture."

"I did," Rhys stated. "And I since learned it was stolen."

"It wasn't fucking stolen," he growled. "And I don't know anything about it. I don't know anything about anybody's car either."

"Really?" the detective asked, eyeing him carefully. "So your name isn't Joland Henge either, right? Colby's brother?"

At that the other guy swore heavily. "That fucking snitch. Andrew's days are numbered too."

"*Too?*" Rhys repeated. "You mean, just like that *damn bitch* whose house you shot into?"

"I didn't shoot no bitch, and I sure as hell don't shoot into houses. You pick up a gun, you use it," he sneered. "Besides, that bitch needs a tune-up."

"Really?" Rhys asked. "And you'll be the one to give it to her?"

"Fuck you. At least I will if she crosses my path. But I don't know nothing about nothing," he told the detective, then crossed his arms and glared at the two men.

Rhys looked over at the detective, one eyebrow raised.

Django nodded. "I've already got a cop car coming to take him in for questioning."

"And what about his buddy Andrew?"

"Oh, he's coming in too. It's definitely a stolen vehicle. And it was found on his property. He's pretty pissed about the whole thing."

"I'm sure he is," Rhys murmured. "Pissed enough to give you this guy's name, right?"

"Absolutely. Nobody likes it when they bring stolen cars to their houses." Django smiled, looking over at Joland. "So we'll see what Andrew's got to say, once you two are nicely tucked in at the station."

"I got a fucking appointment in the morning," Joland declared. "You can't keep me long."

"I can keep you for forty-eight hours if I want to," Django added, still with a smile. "And believe me. Right about now? I want to."

At that, a cruiser pulled up, and they quickly escorted

Joland, swearing and cursing vile threats to everybody and sundry who would listen, into the back.

"Nice character," Rhys said to the detective.

"And what the hell are you doing here?" he asked in exasperation. "I told you that I was coming."

"Yeah, you did, and I was checking to see if you were trustworthy or not."

At that, the detective's eyebrows shot up. "Wow. I can't say I've ever had that happen."

"Let's just say that, in Taylor's case, she's had way more shit go down than any woman should have to encounter, and she has this great fear that authority doesn't give a shit about her. So, for her sake alone, it was important."

The detective considered that and then shrugged. "I guess it makes as much sense as anything right about now, but it's still nothing I'm terribly impressed about."

"Of course, and I wouldn't be at all surprised if you got quite pissed at us," Rhys noted, "but I needed to do it for her sake."

At that, the detective gave a grudging nod. "Fine, but don't fucking doubt my word again."

"I won't have to," Rhys stated. "Now I know that at least you're honorable."

And, with that, he turned to walk back to Taylor. With Tallahassee at his side, he approached his rental truck, frowning when he didn't see her head. As he opened up the driver's door and looked in, there was no sign of her, and he started to swear. "Jesus Christ, Taylor, where are you?" he asked loudly. "I left you for five minutes."

As he turned and looked around, he brought out his phone, calling her. He got no answer. And her phone wasn't ringing.

He turned at the footsteps behind him to find the detective had walked over, a frown on his face. "What's the matter?"

"Taylor was with me," Rhys said. "And now she's gone."

Detective Django pulled out his phone. "I'm calling for a unit. I'll stay here and direct them to you."

Rhys nodded. "Tallahassee and I will start searching now."

CHAPTER 10

TAYLOR WOKE UP to the sounds of somebody close to her, an urgent whisper in her ear.

"Wake up, wake up."

Rhys? She opened her eyes and stared at him groggily. "What happened?" she murmured.

"That's what I would ask you," he said, as he stared down at her.

But even groggy and not sure what was going on, she saw the relief in his expression. He helped her sit up, and she looked around. She was on the grass, beside a bunch of bushes.

He motioned at the bushes beside her. "Tallahassee found you in there."

She looked at the dog and the bushes, then stared at Rhys, uncomprehending.

"Do you have any recollection?"

She thought hard for a moment. And then she nodded slowly. "I was sitting in the truck, waiting. I had just my eyes closed. But my window was open," she admitted, "because it's hot out. And I remember choking, as somebody pulled an arm around my throat and tried to knock me out. I remember fighting back but not getting very far," she murmured. She reached up and touched her throat, wincing. "It hurts to swallow."

"That's it," Rhys declared. "We're taking you to the hospital." She glared at him. He shook his head. "If nothing else, we need to get that throat checked."

"It's fine," she said immediately. He snorted, and she knew that no way he would listen to her now. She groaned. "I can't imagine that it would be serious."

"Maybe not, but I can't take that chance."

She held out her hand. and he slowly stood her on her feet. And noted something on the ground beside her. Rhys picked it up and handed it to her, his face grim. She looked at it in shock. "Really?" she asked, reading the note. *Bitch, layoff.* "Good God," she whispered. She stared at him.

"And you have no way of identifying your attacker, right?"

"I had my eyes open but was facing away from him. Plus I was more concerned about getting free of him," she explained. As she thought about it a bit, she added, "All I could really see was the roof of the cab."

Rhys nodded. "He would have pulled your head back and clamped down against your throat."

"*Great.* Apparently I don't even get peace and quiet just sitting in a vehicle."

"Not anymore," Rhys noted, "and Tallahassee doesn't leave your side again." He helped her slowly walk back to the truck, which was half a block away. "Looks like it was a spur-of-the-moment thing."

"That's what I was thinking," she said. "However, I really don't know. I mean, he had enough wherewithal to hide me in the bushes."

"But he didn't take you with him," Rhys pointed out.

At that, she winced. "Thanks for that thought," she muttered. "I can't imagine that'll be something I care to think about long-term."

"No, it won't be," Rhys agreed, "but, in this case, if he gets another chance, I doubt he'll be so forgiving."

"Forgiving?" She snorted. "Of what? The only thing I can think of is the military investigation. And yet I don't know anything about how it's progressed. In fact, I thought it was closed."

"But just because you don't know doesn't mean that it hasn't gotten to the point where Colby sees he's in trouble."

She thought about that and saw Rhys's truck coming into her view. She sighed in relief. "My leg's really sore too."

He nodded. "After we get through with the hospital visit, we'll take another look at the prosthetic, make sure he didn't damage it."

"He didn't say anything about it, at least I don't remember."

"And that really has no bearing at the moment," Rhys noted. He helped her and Tallahassee into the vehicle and walked around to his side and pulled out his phone. He quickly phoned the detective and told him that he had found Taylor and what she had remembered so far. He added, "I'm taking her to the hospital."

With the detective's voice ringing loud and clear through Rhys's phone, he stated, "I'll meet you there."

She stared at Rhys. "I really don't want to go through all this," she stated.

"It doesn't matter now. This is too far gone for it to ever get washed away anymore. And, of course, I'm more than ever suspicious about your supposed friend."

"You mean, Andrew?"

He nodded. "And then there's also Colby. And his brother Joland."

She nodded. "And Joland was also in military."

"Was he?"

At that, she nodded. "I just forgot about that until now. And I wasn't sure he was involved in this."

"And he might not be, but, from what I'm seeing, he's a possible suspect."

She settled back, her hand gently resting against her throat protectively. "After today, maybe," she murmured.

"Did you ever have much to do with his brother Joland?"

"No," she said, "nothing. He wasn't my kind of guy."

At that, he looked at her and asked, "What does that mean?"

"Rough, arrogant. You know? God's gift to women kind of thing. Whereas I was never drawn to that kind of inflated male ego."

"Aw, c'mon," Rhys teased, with a chuckle. "Are you sure?"

"I'm positive," she murmured, with a smile. "And, no, you don't count."

"Ha. Why don't I count?"

"Because you're not like that," she murmured.

"Are you sure about that?"

"I'm very sure," she declared. "I don't need any other proof than what I've already seen."

"Good," Rhys replied, "then maybe when I tell you to do something, you won't give me quite so much argument."

"I suspect I'll give you even more argument," she said immediately and then managed to smile, before wincing. "I don't suppose you have any water, do you?"

He shook his head. "No, but we'll get you something at the hospital."

He pulled into the parking lot, and she asked, "Are you sure the detective needs to come?"

"After today, yes," he stated. "No way we're not keeping the police in the loop on this one. This is now a physical attack, not just him being an asshole, talking trash, making threats."

"Yeah, whoever it is," she said, with a wave of her hand, "I'd still like to know if Colby's even in town."

"If he is, we'll find out." As they got into the hospital, he took her to Emergency, leaving Tallahassee in the vehicle.

"It's hardly an emergency," she protested.

The receptionist looked at her and asked, "What happened?" He quickly explained, and she told them, "Take a seat. We'll get somebody to check her out."

By the time she sat down, she was called back already. She groaned, as she slowly got vertical again, not sure where the soreness was coming from. Rhys assisted her into a small cubicle. She looked at him and said, "You know that I'll be fine, right?"

"Well, you'll be fine," he declared, "because we won't leave your side again."

She glared at him. "I don't really want a babysitter."

"Doesn't matter what you want at this stage," Rhys said, his tone harsh. "Now be a good girl and let them check you over."

And, with that, a doctor stepped in, and Rhys quickly explained what had happened to her.

The doctor's eyebrows shot up, and he said, "That's not good. Give us a few minutes."

And, with that, Rhys stepped out.

She sat here and spoke to the doctor. She didn't have much information to give him, but, by the time he was done examining her throat and her chest and then her leg, she realized that she'd taken a few hard blows too.

"Honestly it looks like you've had the shit kicked out of you," the doctor noted. "So I'm not sure who this guy is, but that's the last thing we need."

"You and me both," she agreed, her voice soft. "Is that why the prosthetic's so sore?"

"With all the damage that he did, which looks to have been inflicted more as a result of a temper, I'll have to bring the detectives in," the doc told her. "It looks like, while you were down, he just gave you a few hard blows, potentially to teach you a lesson."

She nodded. "Maybe," she noted, her voice soft.

He handed her water and a straw, and she slowly sipped, easing the pain in her throat.

He continued. "I don't see any major damage, so I'll send you home, but I want you to take care, to get off that leg, to watch out for those bruises developing into anything that doesn't look normal," he explained. "If you want some painkillers, I can give you something."

"No, it's not time yet," she said, "I'd just as soon not if I don't have to, anyway."

He smiled. "You've been through too much already. Either people want a lot of them or they tend to not want anything."

"I'd just as soon not have any," she murmured. "Particularly after all the surgeries."

"And I get that," the doc agreed. "Just remember that you don't have to suffer."

"I think I have already been suffering," she murmured.

"And now you don't want to give into it. I get it," he murmured. "I need to see you again in a couple days." She looked at him, startled. He explained, "I just want to check and make sure that there's been no other damage."

"Then maybe we should check for that now," she said in a wry tone.

"I already have," he confirmed, "but some of those bruises are pretty ugly. And some internal damage may show up later."

"And I don't need x-rays?"

He shook his head. "No. You're weight bearing, so I don't expect any broken bones. But I do look for reactions to the hard beating your muscles took." He shrugged. "They'll develop nice and colorful bruises though."

She nodded. "I can handle color."

At that came a voice outside the curtain. It was Rhys.

She replied, "You can come in."

He pulled back the curtain ever-so-slightly, stepped forward, with the detective behind him, and looked at the doc. The doc got Taylor's permission to share her condition with them and quickly explained the rest of her injuries.

"Good God," the detective said, his voice hard. "So it's bad enough that somebody dragged you out of your vehicle and choked you into unconsciousness, but, while you were down, he kicked the crap out of you?"

At that, the doctor nodded. "That's what it looks like."

The detective looked at her to see if she was in agreement.

She shrugged. "I hurt enough for it. I wondered why the pain was so severe. But that makes the most sense." She slowly slid to the floor, gasping.

"Yeah, I want you off that leg," the doctor reminded her. "I'll get a wheelchair for you."

She winced. "No."

He ignored her protests. "*Off the leg* means *off the leg*. It's pretty bruised, and there'll be a fair bit of swelling, and that won't stop for the next couple days. So use crutches again."

"*Great*," she muttered and hoped that nobody would hear.

But, of course, Rhys was close enough that he turned, glared at her, and added, "Yeah, not a problem, Doc. I'll make sure she follows through."

No point in Taylor glaring at Rhys because he was already giving her that look that said he would make good on his promise. And honestly she had no reason to argue with him. She was feeling more amiable than usual. Mostly because she didn't have any energy to handle anything more. The pain had sucked it all away. And she slowly walked toward him, then reached out a hand as the wheelchair came in, and he helped lower her down. As she finally sat in place, she whispered, "Thank God."

"Yeah," Rhys agreed. "If nothing else, this will make sure that you stay off that leg for a bit."

She shrugged. "I was doing my best to stay off of it anyway," she argued, "but now? Well, now I don't really have a whole lot of choice." She looked up at the detective. "Do you need anything from me?"

"I sure do," he said, "but let's get you home. I'll follow and can ask the questions there."

She nodded and let Rhys push her out to the truck.

RHYS PULLED UP in front of her house, let Tallahassee out first, and then came around to her side. Taylor slid off the big bench seat, maybe planning to land on her good leg, but he scooped her up in his arms. Using his good leg to balance on for that moment, he slammed the truck door shut. And carried her right up to the front of the house, ignoring her protests. She finally fell silent, and he nodded. "Good, you're getting it."

She snorted. "You mean, the fact that you're just being all macho?"

"The fact that I care," he corrected her. "And that it really pisses me off that somebody would do this to you. Not only to you but to anybody handicapped."

"And I don't know that he even noticed my prosthetic." He frowned at her. She shrugged. "Honestly, one of the worst nightmares I've ever had is the thought of being attacked, and somebody taking off my prosthetic and throwing it away."

He nodded. "I think anybody in our situation has those kinds of nightmares. In this case, thank heavens that didn't happen."

"Indeed," she murmured.

He set her down slowly onto the couch and asked, "How's this?"

"It's good."

He asked, "Now your crutches are upstairs?" She stared at him. He cocked his head. "Yes, you're using crutches." Her shoulders slumped, as he watched her steadily. "Just for a while, until you get healed."

"Sure." She shrugged. "That's what it starts as. And then—you know yourself—it takes so much longer to build back up again."

"And that's because you haven't stood a chance to get there yet," he argued, with a smile, "but you will."

"I know. I'm just anxious, frustrated, at what appears to

be my lack of progress. And wish I was pissed off, … but that sneak attack was scarier than I want to admit."

"And yet it really isn't because of any lack of progress on your part."

She snorted. "Easy for you to say."

Smiling, he raced up the stairs, found her crutches in the bedroom, then, with a quick glance around to make sure everything was okay, he headed back downstairs. He set them beside her and asked, "Do you need anything to go with this?"

"No," she said. "I'll be fine. It's just, you know, crutches aren't my thing."

"They're nobody's thing," he noted, with a smile.

She laughed at that. "I do need some coffee though. Or at least a bite to eat."

"Or how about just some sleep?" he suggested.

She frowned at that. "Not when we have the detective coming."

He nodded. "That's a good point. I'll go put coffee on." And he walked into the kitchen, and, following her instructions on how to use her maker, he put on a pot of coffee, with enough to give the detective some when he arrived as well. As soon as Rhys was done, he returned to the living room to find her gently massaging her head.

"How's the headache?" he asked.

"It's a bitch," she replied, more vehemently than she thought. And then she sighed. "The doctor offered me painkillers, but I didn't take them."

"That's because you already have some here, I would imagine."

She shrugged. "I do. I was just hoping to not get so attached to them again."

"Did you have problems getting off them?"

She nodded. "They helped me sleep. They helped me get through the days, and I realized that they were just too much help. I wasn't getting back mentally."

"Got it," he noted, "but when you're in pain …"

"Right. It's just that pain ends up being something else very quickly."

"I had a problem for a while there too. I threw them out of the house. And, of course, the next time I sored up my leg," Rhys added, "I was in trouble."

"Right. We do these things because it seems like a good idea at the time, but sometimes I think we end up hating ourselves over it."

"And yet sometimes it's really the best answer."

"Well, I didn't throw them away," she noted. "They're in the downstairs bathroom."

"Do you want anything now?" He turned and looked at her.

She shook her head. "I'll leave off until bedtime."

"Okay, that makes sense too." Hearing a noise, Rhys straightened and looked out the window. "The detective's here."

She nodded. "Good, the sooner we get this over with, the better."

He let the detective in, watching Tallahassee's reaction. He'd learned to respect animals' judgment of character a long time ago. They didn't have the same reasons necessarily for not liking somebody that Rhys might have, but he never discounted it. The detective passed with flying colors, and that was good too.

Django stepped closer to her, looked her over, and asked, "Ma'am, how're you feeling?"

"Like I've had the shit kicked out of me," she said bluntly.

He nodded. "Had that a time or two myself," he shared, "not much fun."

She nodded. "I just wish I understood what was going on."

"That's partly why I'm here," he confirmed. "We need to get to the bottom of this."

"And I get that," she agreed, "but I'm wondering if it isn't from having Rhys around here." Rhys looked at her in surprise. She shrugged. "When you think about it, that's when this all started to go to pot."

"Not quite," he disagreed. "I only happened to be here when that drive-by shooting happened."

She frowned and then conceded that point. "Fine, maybe it wasn't your arrival then." She frowned at that. "I don't know what it was."

"I have an idea though," the detective stated. "I spoke to Jager, and he pulled a few strings—not to get us very much in the way of information because I gather the military doesn't pass on much information," he shared, cocking an eyebrow in Rhys' direction, who immediately nodded.

"Nope, they sure don't."

"But the internal sexual harassment investigation has ramped up, and they've started talking to other people involved in your case, and that would have then brought in more interviews for Colby. They didn't come out and say that they had put him on alert that this investigation was happening right now, but I don't think it takes much to realize that it's potentially all connected."

"I would have assumed it was connected," she agreed. "I just don't quite understand why the assault was done today."

"And that's why I would ask if anything's changed."

"Rhys," she said immediately. "Just Rhys being here."

"Not true," Rhys disagreed. "Yes, I'm a new factor here, but we also went to talk to this *friend* of yours, Andrew."

"Right. And that's the guy I saw today," the detective noted.

"And was he helpful?" Rhys asked.

"Not much. He did give us the address of his friend Joland, once Andrew realized the vehicle Joland drove up in was stolen and was sitting in Andrew's driveway, making him look like a guilty party—or at least connected." Django grimaced. "Andrew got quite pissed about it."

"Yeah, he doesn't like dealing with shitheads," she added, relaxing back into the couch, her eyes closing.

"We can do this another time if you want," the detective stated suddenly.

Her eyes flew open; she looked at him and said, "No, it won't be any better any other time. Better now while it's still fresh."

"And yet I understand that you don't remember much."

She shrugged. "Not much, no." She gave him the same story that she'd told Rhys. "Honestly, once it started, once he grabbed me, I didn't have a chance to do very much at all."

Rhys nodded. While Taylor and the detective talked, and she relayed everything that had happened, Rhys poured coffee for three and brought it to the living room. She hadn't brought up anything new or different—not that he'd expected her to. It just would be nice if there were some sort of understanding of what the hell was going on.

He thought, at the core of it, it was really simple. Somebody was heading for military court, discharge, and potentially serving time. And Rhys was all for it honestly. Assholes like this were not anybody who he wanted to have around her at all. Letting them get away with this crap, when you had the ability to stop it, made you just as bad in Rhys's opinion.

As he set down the coffee, he heard her say something about a smell. He looked at her sharply. "What do you mean, smell?"

She frowned as she thought about it, closing her eyes, her hand instinctively going to her throat. "There was just this smell. I don't even know how to describe it."

"Something like chloroform over your mouth?"

She grimaced. "Well, definitely something was over my mouth, but I thought it was his hand. And, yes, it could have been chloroform." She stared at Rhys. "Why didn't I remember that before?"

He shrugged. "Sometimes the memory does that." He looked over at the detective. "That makes more sense than anything I've heard yet."

The detective looked at him. "In what way?"

"She's a fighter, not the easiest to subdue, and it's hard to strangle somebody sitting in a truck from the outside like that," he explained. "If you think about it, the whole angle of the arm is wrong."

The detective thought about it and slowly nodded. "So you think he used something to knock her out first?"

"If it were me, I would," he confirmed.

She snorted at that. "We keep coming back to the fact that, as far as you're concerned, he did a lot of things that you would do."

"If I were the kind of asshole who would do something like this—to not only a woman but also a disabled woman—

yeah, that's exactly what I would do."

She frowned at that. "And I'm not sure he knew I was disabled."

"If he'd seen your file, or knew anything about you, wouldn't he know?" Rhys asked her.

"Maybe. But maybe he doesn't have that information available," she replied thoughtfully. "And it's not like it's something I have advertised."

"I'm not sure you'd have to. You walk with a limp and a bit of an awkward gait still," he commented. "Although you're getting a lot better, it's not there yet."

She nodded. "I get it and maybe he just—" She stopped, frowned. "Maybe he didn't think I was a threat because of the disability. And maybe he was kicking my leg because he thought it would keep me down," she suggested, holding up her hands, palms out. "He'd be like that."

The detective stepped in and said, "Or he didn't know that you were disabled because he isn't the guy from the military that you have the accusations against."

She nodded slowly. "And that would make sense. Colby may not have told anybody."

"And that could have been just somebody Colby hired on to do this part. Let's go back to that family now," the detective suggested. "Can you explain the relationship between you and these two guys?"

"Three guys, at that," Rhys stated.

At his interruption, she turned to look at him.

"Andrew, Colby, and you knew Colby's brother, Joland, too," he reminded her.

"Yes, but not well," she added, "and he's not somebody that I would have chosen to do anything with."

"Sure, but that just means it's even more important that

we find out how involved he is."

She shrugged. "Okay."

"You don't worry about it," Rhys stated. "That's for the detective to find out."

She laughed at that. "So now it's okay for me to stick my head in the sand?" she teased Rhys.

"Dealing with Colby and Joland are not exactly your thing, right?" the detective asked.

"Nope."

"So now, tell me about these guys," Django said.

She shrugged and led him through what she knew. "Honestly I haven't had anything to do with Andrew at all since I've come back. Whether that's something that's pissing him off, I don't know, but I can't imagine that he would care either way."

"Andrew did open up to you, did he not?" Rhys asked the detective.

At that, the detective nodded. "Once we could prove that the vehicle in his driveway was stolen and that he was either involved or potentially a patsy for whatever was going on, yes. Andrew wasn't happy about it."

"No, I don't imagine he would be," she noted thoughtfully. "He's very much against almost all authority, particularly after his stint in the military. I think he's also very aware of the power of authority, and so he tends to keep a low profile and to stay on the good side of everyone, while operating in the shadows."

"Do you think he's doing anything criminal?"

She stared at him, shrugged, and replied, "I have no idea what he's doing. I don't know what he does for work. I mean, like I mentioned, we lost touch, and he didn't want anything to do with us after his military stint."

"And I find it interesting that he blames you for his time in the military," the detective noted.

"Maybe," she agreed. "I guess he went along because we were going in, but his heart wasn't in it. So I'm not sure why he ended up feeling like he needed to go, but he did."

"Right." The detective nodded and scribbled down more notes.

Rhys sat quietly beside her, listening to her explanation, until a growl came at his feet. He reached a hand down, letting the others talk, and whispered to the dog, "What's the matter, boy?"

At that, Tallahassee straightened up and looked around. Something was obviously bothering him. Rhys got up from the couch and walked with him, following the dog's lead to wherever he decided they needed to go. As it was, the dog appeared to be more concentrated on the back door.

He looked over at her and said, "I'll just take him outside."

She nodded and continued talking with the detective, likely not even registering that Tallahassee was bothered by something. He stepped out to the back door, ever mindful of the bullet that she had found here. And needed to remember to discuss that with the detective as well.

As soon as he got out here, Tallahassee's nose went up, and his growls increased. A whistle came from a distance. His ears twitched. And that brought in an element that Rhys hadn't expected. Somebody was quite comfortable with dogs and either had already made friends with Tallahassee, which wouldn't be good, or was quite comfortable with the idea that he *could* make friends with him. Also not something that Rhys wanted to think about. And then a K9 military connection was also possible. Damn.

Tallahassee, his tail not wagging but definitely uncertain, looked over at Rhys for an order. He immediately put him on guard and walked outside, farther into the backyard. Taylor's property had a fence on all sides, and no gate was on the back. Some acreage was behind the fence but probably not all hers. He studied the area, looking to see where the whistle had come from. When it came again, the dog's tail started to wag. He immediately held him off and made sure that he knew that he was on guard again. With that, the dog settled down and studied the area all around him.

"Seems to be something that you are not sure what to do with," he murmured.

Tallahassee, hearing something in Rhys's voice, looked up at him and whined.

"It's all right, boy. We just have some work cut out for us."

But it was necessary work, if he would look after Taylor. Not that Taylor would be all that happy to be *looked after*. He smiled at the thought because she would be just that much crankier about not wanting to have a guard around, and yet she needed him. Tallahassee remained definitely uncertain, while Rhys studied the surrounding darkness, looking for movement, looking for anything that would give him an idea of where this person was, who obviously was known to Tallahassee.

As he watched, a shadow slowly detached itself in the far distance. Rhys sank down a bit farther behind the wooden fence, waiting to see how bold this guy would be. He was pretty bold, as he soon hopped the fence and came toward Tallahassee. Rhys watched the dog carefully. However, now understanding that this wasn't necessarily a friend, Tallahassee was on guard and watched him carefully.

When the man called out to him, he didn't use Tallahassee's name, which was good because that would mean that this guy didn't know Taylor enough to realize what the dog's name was.

Rhys continued to watch the stranger, who walked slowly closer to Tallahassee. Rhys waited, until the intruder was just about at the War Dog. Rhys crouched down low and waited, and, just as he was about to pounce, a light went on in the kitchen, and a voice called out.

The detective was looking for him.

And, just like that, the intruder raced back and jumped the fence and took off. Soon Rhys heard a vehicle in the distance driving away, and he swore, realizing once again his intruder had gotten away. He bolted to his feet in time to see the detective step out. He glared at Django. "I was just about to catch an intruder."

The detective frowned at him.

Rhys continued. "He came over the back fence, whistling to the dog and talking to him."

"Did he have a weapon?"

"Not that I could see, no," Rhys noted in disgust. "But you called out just at the time, and he heard you, and he bolted out over the back fence. A vehicle took off right away after that."

"Did you get a look at him?"

He shook his head. "It's too dark. But, speaking of which, did she tell you about the bullet?"

"She gave me her version of it, yes," he replied. "The trouble is, we obviously have something going on here that we're not too sure what's happening."

"You think?" he quipped, shaking his head. "This is just … All of it's just too stupid."

"And I get that," Django agreed. "Sorry for my timing."

"Whatever," he muttered. He looked back over to search the trees and the encroaching darkness. "Is she still sitting down?"

"Yeah, she looks pretty tired. I was looking to let you know that I was leaving and to make sure that you stayed close."

"Oh, I'll be staying close. Damn close now." The two men stared out in the distance. "I don't understand what he's after though."

"I think just to terrorize her," Django suggested. "There's something in her chart about being unstable after her accident."

Rhys snorted at that. "I wonder why? She goes to the military, to the authorities, with a story of sexual harassment. And gets the runaround."

"And I think she's holding back something about that too," Django added, glancing over at him.

"She said she wasn't raped," Rhys stated.

"No, but, as we know, an awful lot of other things can happen."

He winced and nodded. "I know. If I get a chance to get her to open up enough, I might ask more questions. However, the bottom line is, she went to the people who she thought were there to protect her, and instead she feels like they betrayed her. Meanwhile, in the process, she was labeled as unstable."

"After the injury and the therapy, I'm sure that didn't help."

"No, it wouldn't have." Rhys swore at that. "It just pisses me right off to think that, whether this guy knows that she's disabled or not, for her, it ups the level of anxiety tenfold.

And I suspect he's doing what he can to make it even worse."

The detective nodded, his face grim. "You know what? When the assholes come out of the woodwork, it never ceases to amaze me just how rotten people can be."

"Well, I won't be leaving her alone until this is resolved," Rhys declared.

The detective looked at him. "And just what is your relationship with her?"

He frowned at him. "We're friends now, but I came to find the War Dog and to make sure he was okay and in good hands." He glanced at Tallahassee, who was even now walking up and down the back porch, like he needed to go out to the bathroom. "I'll take him out now, if you want to hang around for a minute," Rhys noted, "and then I will come back in and look after her." And, with that, he took the dog out, the detective standing watch on the porch.

As soon as they were done, he and the dog joined Django on the back porch. "Thanks. I'll go in and talk to her."

He nodded. "You do that, although she might even be asleep."

"She didn't want to fall asleep until she'd had her painkillers," he shared.

"Unless the stress, the trauma of the day, had its way with her regardless."

Rhys winced at that. "I could imagine, not to mention she was dealing with headaches."

"And, of course, she probably doesn't like painkillers." He looked over at him. The detective shrugged. "I've been hurt on the job too," he added. "We tend to go one way or the other. We like them too much, or we don't like them at all."

"Like most of us," Rhys said, "I think I have been both

ways, one after the other."

The detective's eyes lit up with understanding. "Very true. I wouldn't want anything to happen to her, so I like knowing that you're staying close by for the next few days."

"Yeah, I'm not leaving," he repeated, "not until this is solved."

And, with that, he walked the detective to the front door and said, "Good night."

He headed back into the living room, and, sure enough, she'd fallen asleep.

CHAPTER 11

W HEN TAYLOR WOKE the next morning, she found
herself half-dressed under the covers on her bed. She
lay here for a long moment, trying to figure out just what
had happened. There was no panic, but, at the same time, a
disquiet filled her that she wasn't used to. Her mind filtered
back to the attack of the previous night and realized that she
had likely fallen asleep on the couch. And that naturally
followed into the next step, which logically should have been
Rhys himself carrying her up the stairs.

She winced at that. She was definitely not used to somebody taking over, and she certainly wasn't used to anybody
having the ability to carry her up a set of stairs, but he'd
already demonstrated he was perfectly capable and willing to
do it, if needed.

And then she realized her prosthetic was off as well. Her
breath released with a slow sigh. He'd left her in panties and
a bra and a T-shirt but had taken off her prosthetic, knowing
himself just how hard it would be to sleep and how sore she
would be the next day. She reached down a hand and gently
smoothed it over the edge of her skin. It was definitely puffy
and tender.

She didn't know how she felt about what he'd done, and
yet she couldn't in any way judge him for it because she
knew that, from his perspective, it was the right thing to do.

And how did you blame your guardian angel for being an angel? She sighed, sat up, took off the rest of her clothing, grabbed her crutches, and made her way to the shower.

After a quick shower—where she scrubbed her hair several times—she made her way back into the bedroom and dressed. Of course not having to put on the prosthetic saved her some time and energy, and she slowly made her way to the top of the stairs. It was one of the reasons she absolutely detested crutches was because of the stairs. They just weren't built for people like her. And yet it was what she had to deal with.

She had done so as well before, just not with that same understanding that she would still do it again. Using the railing with one hand and her crutch with the other, she slowly made her way downstairs. She half expected him to come into the living room, scoop her up, and save her that trip too, but she was glad when he didn't.

When she got into the kitchen, he sat at the table, waiting for her.

He looked up, smiled, and asked, "Hey, did you get some sleep?"

She nodded self-consciously. "Yes, thank you."

He shrugged. "I could hardly leave you asleep on the couch. You had a pretty rough evening as it was."

She nodded. "And you're right. I wouldn't have slept very well at all on the couch." She made her way over, poured herself a cup of coffee, and looked at him. "What about you?"

"I did. I grabbed some sleep. I've already taken Tallahassee out." He walked over and picked up her cup and carried it to the table.

She winced. "At times like this I realize I may not be the

best person to have a dog," she admitted. "It didn't even cross my mind that he needed to go out."

"He would need to on a regular basis. You might want to consider putting in a doggie door for him," he suggested. "But you don't need to make that decision right now."

She slumped onto the chair beside him at the table. "I think I'd make a terrible dog owner," she murmured.

"I don't think so. You just need things adjusted for you and him. Like an automatic dog feeder too," he added. "Remember. What they really need is love and caring first. I personally like the doggy door option, so he can come and go at will."

She stared at him. "Did you walk him?"

"I did," he confirmed, "but, in the case of your condition right now, you could have just opened the door and let him loose out into the backyard."

She nodded. "I guess that would have done in a pinch."

"Absolutely would have," he agreed, with a smile.

He studied her face, and she saw the concern in his gaze. "I'm feeling fine," she murmured.

"Really though?"

She nodded, with a smile this time. "Really. No lasting effects."

"Well, that's good news. It's bad enough that you were attacked at all. The fact that you were attacked on my watch just makes me even angrier."

And she realized that he was taking the blame. "Whoa, whoa, whoa," she said, frowning at him. "This is not your fault."

"Are you sure?" he asked, with a hard look. "Because, from my calculations, it sure as hell looks like it's my fault."

"I don't want you thinking that," she stated. "You're

here to help me, and, if we stirred up a hornet's nest, well, we stirred it up. Maybe it needed to be stirred up."

"Maybe," he said. "Doesn't make me feel any better."

She sighed. "Let's just say it was a bad deal for both of us."

He laughed at that. "If you want to say it that way, sure. What you don't know is, while I was out with Tallahassee last night, the detective came to find me, but his timing sucked. I was just waiting to jump an intruder, who hopped over the fence to get close to Tallahassee."

She stared at him in shock. "What?"

He nodded. "Somebody was coming into your backyard, having already whistled at the dog a couple times. The dog was very confused, particularly when I gave him the order to stand guard. But the end result was, I didn't get the asshole because of the detective's timing."

"Well, shit. No wonder you didn't get any sleep."

His look turned wry. "And here I told you that I had a good night."

"Yeah, you don't lie well either."

He burst out laughing. "See? We're really getting to know each other."

"We definitely are. That doesn't mean that we're that close yet," she murmured.

"We have time," he noted comfortably. She looked at him in surprise. He grinned. "I promised the detective I was sticking around until this is resolved." She frowned at that. He reached out, tapped her fingers gently, and added, "Besides, I was planning on doing it anyway."

She shook her head. "You don't need to feel responsible for me."

"I don't," he stated, with a smile, "but I won't leave anybody in trouble, and, in this case, I'm still working on Tallahassee."

She wasn't sure what to say to that. The fact that she wanted him to use other excuses revealed a lot about her own mind-set. She looked over at him. "Did you eat?"

He shook his head. "No, I didn't. I was waiting for you."

She smiled. "And here I figured you'd have had breakfast already cooked for me."

His grin flashed. "Say the word," he shared, "and I'll be up and cooking in a heartbeat."

"*Word*," she replied immediately. He burst out laughing, and she grinned at him. "It's nice to feel laughter again," she noted. His gaze was full of understanding. It was so odd to know that somebody out there understood what she was going through. Maybe not everything but certainly in terms of dealing with a prosthetic. "Did—" She stopped.

"Did what?"

She shrugged. "I guess I was just asking about what support system you had during recovery, but you've already pretty well mentioned the good VA center group you experienced. I was thinking that, for myself, it's very—It's nice to know that you understand."

"Ah." He nodded. "You're right, and I think that was a benefit I had where I was. And you missed out on that, so what seems like normal to me is something extra special to you."

She nodded. "I guess. … Just seems so strange to think that our experiences could have been so different."

"I think it's also based on how we recovered mentally," he noted, "not that you needed longer to recover." He tried to quickly cover his tracks.

She lifted a hand and waved off his correction. "I'm not

sure that I didn't though because I was still dealing with all the military stuff. I definitely sensed not having any support, not having any direction to go to for help. And I, … I would not wish that on anybody."

"No," he murmured. "That doesn't add anything good to the experience."

She burst out laughing. "No, you got that right."

She watched as he hopped up, walked to the fridge, and asked, "What do we have to eat?"

"I hope you planned for breakfast when you bought groceries earlier," she murmured.

"I did. A good reason why I should cook then. If I brought it into the house, I should at least cook it." He pulled out sausages and a dozen eggs and bread and asked, "Will this do for you?"

"Absolutely, and I am really hungry."

"Good, I don't know any better way to heal than eating good food, outside of rest and stacking up on the vitamins and minerals. You need the energy that comes from food."

"I'll take whatever excuses you want to make," she replied, with a smile.

At that, he got to work, and she watched how efficiently he worked in the kitchen.

"I do like to cook," she shared, "but I haven't done a whole lot of it, and then, of course, since I got back, it's been more of a challenge than I had expected."

"That's because you still haven't adapted," he replied. "There's more to adapting to this new world than just being able to walk. So much else goes into our lives that we have to adapt to."

"I get it, and I've been working on it." A yawn escaped her. He frowned at her, and she shrugged. "I just seem to always be tired now."

"And, in that case," he noted, "it's a good thing I am cooking because you need to rest, even if that takes a week or two."

"I've never really known how to do that," she murmured.

"Well, I'm here to show you," he said, with a big grin.

"Oh, so now you'll cook and clean for me?"

He shrugged. "If I need to, yeah. Sure. Why not? It's not like I have anything better to do."

"And you're still trying to avoid going home, right?"

"I won't be going home in the same capacity at all," he noted. "That is for sure."

"You got that much decided?"

"Oh, absolutely. I just needed to get out and to get some distance to figure out what my next step was."

"And when you do find that," she said, "let me know."

"Well, the next step is that I'm staying here," he stated firmly. "We'll go from there afterward."

"That's not a very big next step," she told him, frowning. "A lot of people would say that was not even a step, and that was more like a sidestep."

He burst out laughing, as he turned the sausages in the pan, and looked back at her with a grin. "I like that we can joke. When I think I'm doing better than I am, you're right there to pull me back to reality. And when you think that you're doing worse than you are, I'm right there to let you know that you're doing just fine."

She grinned. "So what does that make us? A match made in heaven?"

"No, not necessarily," he replied, making her pause, "but it does mean that we're doing just fine together."

"It does, indeed," she agreed, with a smile. And then she stopped, her smile falling away.

"*Uh-oh*," he said. "Now what is it?"

She looked at him and then shrugged. "I just never thought—I mean, it's not really appropriate."

"Oh no you don't," he said. "Remember? We can talk."

"Right, but I'm not so sure about this."

"You mean, relationships?"

She stared at him, dumbfounded. "How did you know?"

"Because I think that's one of the other things that so many of us struggle with afterward. How we're now ugly, deformed, in some way less than we were before."

"Well, we are," she stated. "I mean, as a weight loss program, it's not one I would recommend, but I'm definitely a lot less than I was before."

He grinned. "And it's not something that you should be worried about. … And, no, I haven't had a relationship since I lost my limb. And being at home with my parents fawning all over me is not exactly independence-inducing."

She groaned. "Oh, that's so true." She gave him a knowing smile. "I mean, our parents can sometimes be great, but, at the same time, they can be overwhelming."

"And in my case," he noted, "they came from love, so that wasn't a problem. However, their version of love was a little bit too smothering for me. My father was happy when I left, more for my sake than for his."

"And your mother?"

"Devastated," he replied immediately.

"I think moms are supposed to be," she said. "They want to keep us safe and locked away, so that we won't go through anything terrible. Yet, at the same time, we can't protect ourselves all the time, and terrible things happen to good people."

He looked at her in appreciation. "And you need to re-member that because, for all your parents' mistakes and for what they did or did not do, I suspect that they still loved you."

"I think they did too. They just didn't know how to get out of themselves to the point that they could care enough about others." She shrugged. "I've put my parents behind me. They are not an issue anymore."

"And I'm glad to hear that. So what is your issue?"

"Still a lack of self-confidence in where I'm at," she admitted immediately. "A lack of confidence in the future—how I'll survive, how I'll handle various aspects of this new world. I would have always thought that I was good at adapting. Yet this makes me take another look at that assumption."

"Right," he agreed. "You're adapting because you have to right now. However, that doesn't mean that that'll be an easy thing to continue."

"Right." She could smile at that reality right now. She watched as he cracked the eggs, tossed them into a bowl, and scrambled them. "I guess it's just all about time."

"That's exactly what it is," he said, with a nod. "It's just a matter of time. And everything's new and different, but the second time you do it, then it's not so new, and it's not so different. What we don't need is this asshole, who's making your life even more difficult and making you even more insecure."

"No. I was thinking about him, when I woke up this morning," she shared. "Not that I have anything else to help identify him in any way, but that sensation that he was there and out to get me—whether he knew I was disabled or not wasn't the point. I knew I was feeling insecure, so I was reacting from that point of view."

"Maybe," Rhys stated, "and maybe you just didn't have a chance to do anything but fight for your life. Reacting is what we do when we're struggling to survive, and, if you want to pick up more self-defense courses, I think that's a great idea—if only to make yourself feel better."

She pondered that. "I guess if I took on some updated defense courses," she noted, "it wouldn't be a bad idea."

"No, and it would be better if you found somebody who was also disabled, who could help you realign your weight distribution for some of those moves. I'm sure you have quite a bit of self-defense training already from being in the military."

"I do," she said, with a nod. "But, just when you start to think that that is of any value, someone strangles me, and that reminds me that the previous training is not enough. Sad to see how easy it is to become a victim."

"Right," he agreed, giving her a warm smile. "And there'll always be something like that out there." He quickly served up breakfast and pulled the toast from the toaster and brought it over for her to butter.

"You're also very easy to talk to," she murmured.

"I like that we can talk and can be truthful with each other." He looked over to see Tallahassee sliding closer to her plate. "And one word to the wise. Don't feed him at the table."

She looked down, saw the dog sneaking up closer, and smiled. "Except for on special occasions."

"Yeah, when would those be?" he asked curiously.

"Well, if he ever saves me or does something equally brave."

"Well, in that case, all bets are off. I don't think there's a dog owner in the world who wouldn't spoil them silly at that point."

She smiled. "I think all animals should have a right to get spoiled and to be loved. I feel like Tallahassee obviously lost out on that not too long ago."

They ate in peace, and then, when she was just about done, he asked, "What do you want to do today?"

She smiled. "Relax. Stay at home. Do nothing."

"Perfect. So then I bought enough steaks that I want to barbecue again. Are you up for that?"

She nodded immediately. "Absolutely," she murmured. "But we had steak already."

"Yeah, I want to do these differently," he said, with a big grin.

"If you say so. I gather you are a red meat eater."

"In a big way." He nodded. "What do you want to go with it?"

She shrugged. "Honestly I'm totally happy to have whatever it is you're thinking of."

"Well, that makes it easy."

"I'm all about easy," she murmured. She sagged back and said, "I'm already getting hungry, Just thinking about steaks again."

And, with that, he got up, pulled the steaks from the fridge, added a bunch of spices together, and rubbed them with the mixture.

"If I wasn't quite so tired, I would like to know what you're doing."

"And I'm happy to teach you on the next round," he said instantly.

She thought about it for a long moment and then asked,

"Are you planning on staying long?"

He washed his hands, stuck the steaks into the fridge. Then walked over, sat down beside her, and asked, "Is that a problem?"

"It is if you're trying to hide from your family," she noted cautiously.

He looked at her in surprise and then chuckled. "You know what? Of all the things that my parents are, they're not somebody to run from," he said. "I was just looking for a reason to leave, to break that bond, so that I could get back to my own life. Staying here would not be to avoid going home."

She smiled, feeling something inside herself settle.

He added, "It would, however, be because I would like to get to know you better." She stared at him in astonishment. He smiled. "And don't tell me that you don't feel it too."

She shrugged. "Well, I feel something. It's just been—" She winced. "It's just been a long time, and I wasn't sure what I was reading for body language."

"And that's okay." He smiled. "Really. It is totally okay because I would expect something like that anyway. Life hasn't been the easiest for either of us. I think I understand exactly where you're coming from, and, right now, I don't want to see you fending off these assholes alone."

"But I don't want to be a charity case either," she stated immediately.

He looked at her and shook his head. "Absolutely no way would that happen. No, not at all," he murmured. "And see? We can talk about anything that bothers you."

"We *can* talk," she agreed. "And when you say that you'd like to get to know me better, what does that mean?"

He looked at her and grinned. "I like who you are. I re-spect where you're at, and I really like the fact that there's this chemistry between us. It feels like a very long time since I've felt anything like that."

He studied her face intently and she felt heat washing through her.

He nodded. "You feel it too, and that's good. It's sup-posed to be that way."

"Yeah, it just doesn't always work out that way," she murmured.

"Nope, it doesn't, but that doesn't mean that this time there isn't something special happening. And that is only if you're willing to take a chance," he noted.

Something was in his voice. Still unsure of how far to push it, she murmured, "I guess I'm just wondering whether this is something that we're really seriously working on or that you're just kind of joking about."

He scooted his chair closer to her, held her hands. "I'd like to see where it goes," he said. "Obviously we don't know each other very well, but"—he shrugged, gave her a small smile—"I haven't found anybody half as interesting as you in a very long time."

A smile peeked out, even though she tried hard to con-trol it. But inside she was absolutely delighted. She reached out and gently stroked his face. "Well, I already know that you can handle things in a difficult situation. You make a hell of a hero."

His eyes widened in horror. "No, no, no, no, don't call me that."

She burst out laughing. "And here I thought guys liked to be thought of as the heroes."

"I don't know about other guys, but I'm just me, just a

man."

"Oh, I don't think there's anything very simple, *or just*, about you," she murmured. "It was a very strange feeling to wake up this morning in bed."

He winced at that. "I know. I'm sorry. I was wondering just what I should do about it, but I knew you wouldn't sleep comfortably down here."

"And that's fine." She put her fingers to his lips to stop the words from pouring out. "It's just … For the first time in a very long time I felt like somebody gave a crap."

He nodded. "And I get that too," he agreed, with a sigh. "Sometimes it feels like we're the only ones in the world, and nobody understands."

"Exactly." She nodded. "And the thing is, you do understand, and that's a very unique experience for me right now."

"Just don't mistake any feelings that you might have as being gratitude."

"Oh, I'm not that foolish." She laughed. "I have an awful lot of common sense in my system. If anything, I would overemphasize that you aren't to be trusted."

He winced at that.

"But, as I've come to understand, you're a very different kettle of fish."

"I am," he declared, "but, if you keep making food references, you'll make me hungry again."

She grinned at him. "And I love the fact that we can laugh."

He nodded. "That's what I meant about talking and laughing and just enjoying being together," he murmured. "So I suggest that we spend the next few days getting to know each other on a deeper level."

"I'm totally okay with that, as long as whoever is doing

this to me lets us have that time."

"We'll take the time," he stated, "because I don't know about you, but I don't have anything more pressing to worry about on my plate. Having found you, I can't say that I'm too eager to let anybody else get their hands on you."

"Well, that's good to hear," she said, "because, man, that would suck. I've been to hell and back already. I really don't want to let this asshole get a piece of me."

"You mean, *another* piece of you."

She winced. "Sure, bring that up."

He grinned at her. "Remember? We get to talk about anything, and, in this case, he won't get another piece of you."

"At least as far as you can help it," she murmured.

"Right," he agreed. "And, yes, there are always extenuating circumstances that none of us want to think about because shit can still happen, even when we thought everything else was good."

She nodded. "You know what? If I'd had any idea that that vehicle would blow to high hell"—she shook her head—"I'd have stayed home that day. I knew Colby was behind it, but I never could get the MPs to look at it. They told me that they would do an investigation, but they highly doubted that Colby would have had anything to do with the explosion."

"And what do you think?"

"I think it was him because that fits what I have in my head of him. That's probably not fair. And I'm not so pressed to make his life miserable that I would try to believe something that doesn't make sense."

"And you never heard what the accident was caused by?"

"Apparently gas," she said, with a shrug, "but it's not as

if I had anything on me that was flammable. And I don't know where a spark could have come from to have set it off."

"Right," he murmured. "And were you alone?"

"More or less," she replied. "A few people were around the warehouse, but I'm not too sure if anybody was closer than that."

He frowned, as he thought about it. "You're thinking about him again."

"Sure, because, I mean, that's another extreme, but I wouldn't put it past him. Everything he's done so far has been pretty extreme." She frowned, as she thought about it. "I don't even know if he was there or not that day. He probably wouldn't have let me see him if he was."

"No, I don't imagine he would have. If you think about it, that's not too far out of the realm of possibility though."

With the two of them in accord, they spent the rest of the day checking up on the outside world, contacting the detective, getting an update from Rhys's bosses on the status of her case with the military, and generally just enjoying each other's company.

When nothing else happened that day, she smiled and said, "Maybe you scared them off."

He nodded. "I'd hope so. Otherwise I'd be afraid I'm losing my touch."

She snickered at that. "I don't know about your touch, but it's quite possible."

He lunged toward her in mock laughter. And she jolted backward, trying to evade him, she ended up almost toppling to the ground.

He caught her midfall, picked her up, swung her around, and sat down with her in his arms. "See? I won't let anything happen to you."

Still stunned at the speed by which it all had shifted in her world, she looked over at him, smiled, and wrapped her arms around his neck. "You know what? I think I might just believe you."

He chuckled. "And so you should. I don't lie."

"I'm glad to hear that," she murmured. "Believe me. I've had enough of liars in my lifetime."

"Your family?"

She nodded. "Yes, they definitely had some issues."

"Of course they did, but those aren't your issues anymore," he noted. "It's time for a whole new lifestyle."

"I get it," she murmured.

He looked around and asked, "Have you got any plans for this place?"

"Lots," she said, "at least in the rental world. However, I need to continue to heal and to not take on too much more."

"Got it," he agreed.

"Unless"—she looked over at him and grinned—"unless you have any experience with renovations."

"Sure," he confirmed, with a smile. "But we'd be signing up for quite a few months together."

"Oh, that's too bad." Then she chuckled. "Of course I'm teasing, but there hasn't been anything problematic between us so far."

"Except for when I tell you to jump."

"Yeah, I'll never really be good at that," she replied immediately. "So, if you're looking for somebody to jump on command, you probably should find somebody else." As she went to get off his lap, he snagged her and pulled her close and said, "I don't want anybody else. Matter of fact, all I can think about is how much I want you."

And pulling her closer, he slowly lowered his head, giving her every chance to pull away. And, when his lips pressed hard against hers, all coherent thoughts fled.

WHAT RHYS THOUGHT was a simple testing of the waters ended up taking him into a burning conflagration and back, as she threw her arms around his neck and responded with a passion that he'd never expected. When he finally managed to pull his head back, he was out of breath and gasping. One look at her dazed expression and he knew that it had hit her exactly the same way.

He stared down at her and muttered, "Well, I wasn't exactly planning that."

She wrapped her arms tighter around his neck. "Yeah? So what were you planning?" she asked, as she reached up and kissed him on her own right.

He pulled her tight, kissing her back, realizing that, since it had been a long time for him, he either needed to stop teasing—although it was damn nice to be able to—or they would take this further. But he was afraid that would be too soon for her.

She pulled her head back, looked at him, and asked, "Second thoughts?"

"Oh, not, … not at all. … I just didn't want to push you, if you weren't ready."

She snorted. "Like I haven't wasted enough time already." He looked at her in surprise. She shrugged. "I didn't have any relationships in the military because of *him*. And then, after the injury, I didn't think relationships would be in my future."

He winced at that. "You know something? We really

need to work on that."

"I thought that's what we were working on." And then she chuckled. "But, hey, if you're too scared …"

Immediately he pulled her tightly into his arms, lowered his head, and seared one into her soul. When she was left gasping, he asked, "Does that tell you how scared I am?"

"Hey," she murmured against his lips, "I know it's not quite dinnertime yet, so we could take this upstairs."

He closed his eyes, dropped his forehead against hers, and whispered, "You sure?"

She pinched him hard. He looked at her in surprise. "Don't ask that again. I do know my own mind, and I certainly know my own body. And right now it wants something that's right in front of it. It's like having a chocolate sundae that I know I can have, as long as I convince you of it."

He looked at her and started to laugh. "Well, that is the first time I've been compared to a chocolate sundae," he noted.

"Get used to it." She grinned. "Who knows what I might compare you to next?"

He rolled his eyes and stood, with her wrapped up in his arms. "In that case, I suggest we take this upstairs." And he walked calmly and steadily toward the stairs.

She wrapped her arms around his neck and whispered, "Are you sure I'm not too heavy?"

"Nope, absolutely not—although you probably should have grabbed your crutches."

"That's fine. If I need to come back down later," she said, "I'll scooch down on my butt."

He laughed at that. "Oh my, the image that brings up …"

"I know. It kind of made me laugh too. Yet I've done it before."

"I have too," he confirmed, with a nod. "You know something? You do what you gotta do."

Upstairs he walked into the master and said, "Pull back the blankets," and he tilted her ever-so-slightly. She grabbed a corner of the blankets and ripped them off the bed. And then with one fell swoop, he dropped her gently into the center of the bed.

"Now that," she said, "was a trip worth waiting for." She sat up and quickly stripped off her clothes, even as he did the same.

He shook his head. "We should be taking our time with this. There's no rush."

"But there is a rush," she disagreed, "and you need to hurry." He gave a bark of laughter, as she immediately pulled her head from her T-shirt and gazed up at him impudently. "Besides, unless you're just a one-time kind of guy, we have all night, if not several days' worth ahead of us."

"Hey, I'd like to see several weeks' worth," he noted.

"Or months or years," she added, stopping and looking at him.

"Or years." He nodded. "I don't know about you, but, when you find what's right, it's right."

She smiled, reached behind her, unclipped her bra, threw it across the bed, and quickly stripped off her jeans. And there she was in a thong, sitting and waiting for him. He whistled hard, feeling his muscles strain, as he struggled to get his sock and his jeans off at the same time. He fumbled and fell to the side of the bed, swearing. But her laughter made it just that much better. He looked at her and grinned. "See? A little too eager."

"Glad to hear it," she said gently. "I'd hate to think I'm all alone in this."

"Never," he replied, as he finally managed to get everything off. He looked down at his prosthetic and quickly unclipped it and then rolled the sock off his stump. "Now look at us, a matched set," he said, with a big grin.

She opened her arms and whispered, "And honestly I'm devastated for your sake, but, for my sake, right now? I'm delighted."

He nodded in understanding, knowing exactly where she was coming from. "But you know something?" he added, as he shifted higher up on the bed, pulling her over until she lay on top of him. "You talk too much." And, with that, he flipped her so she was under him, and he lowered his head and kissed her.

CHAPTER 12

TAYLOR HAD NEVER felt like this, or maybe it had just been so long that she didn't know it was even possible to feel like this. But, as his hands stroked and his lips teased and his tongue tormented, she was shivering within minutes. When he gently ran a hand down over her stump, she froze, her gaze flying up to his. He just stared down at her, and then lifted her leg and kissed the end of her stump.

She shuddered, crying out.

"I know. They're amazingly sensitive, aren't they?" he asked, doing it again and again.

She shivered in his arms, whispering, "That's just ..." And she didn't have a word for it. But he understood.

He leaned over, taking her with his lips, and shifted until he was in position. "I know," he said. "And sometimes some things are just that much better together." And he pulled her gently beneath him and rested right there.

She smiled, looping her arms over his neck. "I didn't think it could be like this."

He nodded. "And honestly it's been so long for me that I'd forgotten."

"I hear you," she murmured and then wiggled beneath him. "Shouldn't you be doing something?"

He smiled against her lips. "Soon." He whispered, "Very soon," as he slid a hand down to cover her breasts, and then he leaned over and took the nipple in his mouth and suckled hard. She arched underneath him, crying out as he then moved to the other breast to give it the same ministration. By the time he ran a light tongue down to her belly button, where he dropped a kiss and then one on her hip bone, she was grabbing him by the hair and pulling him up toward her.

"Now," she demanded, twisting beneath him.

And, with a groan, he complied, seating himself deep within her.

She shuddered beneath him, her eyes closed.

"Are you all right?" he asked, worry in his tone.

She smiled, opened her gaze, and whispered, "Never better." She wrapped her arms around his neck and added, "I so missed this."

He started to move, slowly at first, as if gauging her reaction, and then faster and faster as passion overtook them both. And, when she came apart in his arms, he followed soon afterward, leaving her quaking, as she held him close, her heart full, her mind completely overwhelmed with what had just happened. As he shifted his weight and came down beside her and held her close, she whispered, "Wow."

"Double wow," he murmured back and pulled her even tighter against him, just rocking gently in place.

She looked up, opened her mouth, and then no words came out. Yet she felt a tear forming at the corner of her eye.

He leaned over, licked away the tear, and whispered, "Are you okay?"

She nodded. "Absolutely, I'm okay." She tightened her arms around him and added, "It's just so overwhelming." He nodded. "Just that we've crossed that threshold, both of us," she said, placing her injured and still sore leg up against his own shortened limb. "And to think that we could find each other."

"I know. Sometimes you wonder if things aren't meant to be," he murmured.

She nodded immediately. "It did cross my mind. Either it was that or you're some sort of wizard."

He burst out laughing. "I don't know about that. You're definitely magic though for me."

She smiled, leaned up, kissed him gently. "You know what? I wouldn't mind doing that again."

He looked at her wide-eyed and whispered, "Oh, now that would be my pleasure." And he flipped her beneath him and started all over again.

When she opened her eyes again, she realized that she'd fallen asleep. He was dozing gently at her side. She shifted and stood up slowly and remembered she didn't have her crutches, but, using the bed, she hopped her way gently to the bathroom.

When she came out, he was sitting up and noted, "You do that pretty well."

"Lots of practice," she stated. "I never did take to the crutches."

"Me neither," he agreed, "but they're, … they're a necessary evil."

"And honestly I will admit that sometimes they're just a relief to get the pressure off the leg too."

He smiled. "Outside of the pain of having to get dressed, how about dinner?"

"I could use food," she said immediately.

He grinned. "See? Now I really like that. You have an honest appetite, and you never ever turn me down on food."

"And I won't either," she stated. "It's been a side effect

of getting injured that I'm always hungry. Before I, … I didn't have any appetite because I was dealing with the stress of him coming up behind me at any point in time."

At that comment, Rhys frowned, and she immediately added, "But, since I got into the accident and woke up needing to heal, I'm always hungry."

"Well, maybe that's a good thing," he replied slowly. He hopped up, grabbed his boxers, put them on, and then slowly rolled the sock back onto his stump and affixed his prosthetic. He grabbed his T-shirt, threw it over his head, and asked, "What do you need to get downstairs?"

She shrugged. "I can get there on my butt," she said. "But, before I do that, I want a little bit of clothing to protect from any rug burns."

He nodded. "Sounds good." And he waited for her to put on panties and a pair of shorts, then added her bra and T-shirt. "It's such a shame to cover all that up."

She gave him a teasing smile. "Well, I could take it off again, but we might never eat then."

"Good point," he said. "Food first."

And, with that, she added, "My crutches are downstairs, so it'll have to be hopping for me."

He reached out a hand, and, using him for support, she made her way to the top of the stairs, and then, laughing, she sat down and slowly bumped her way down. He was at the bottom, waiting for her. He reached out a hand, and she laughed and accepted it.

"You know what? There's such a stigma about accepting help at one point in time in the recovery journey," she shared. "I was getting pretty stuck on it myself."

"I noticed," he said.

She smiled. "But it's not so bad with you."

"I think that's because you know I've been there," he offered. "I'm not coming from a position of ego or anything else. It's just a case of I've been there. I know how hard it is. So, if you want my help, my help is here."

She nodded. "And that makes it so much easier."

And, with his help again, she made her way into the kitchen, where she grabbed her crutches. "Now I'm good."

He laughed. "And a few minutes ago you were telling me that you hated crutches."

She smiled. "That's very true."

And then a strange voice called out, "About time you got downstairs."

As she turned, Colby sat at the dining room table, a gun held to the detective. She stared at him in shock, her mind racing to process the scene. And then she turned, as she realized something else. Tallahassee was missing. And immediately guilt struck her heart. "If you've killed my dog …" she said, her voice deadly soft.

"Yeah, what?" he asked, with a sneer. "I'm holding a gun to a cop. You really think a dead dog will make any damn bit of difference to me?"

She went to lunge forward, but Rhys held her back. "Wait."

"Yeah, obey your new handler," Colby taunted. "What the hell are you doing, messing up my life right now."

"Me?" she repeated, staring at him. "I didn't even know you were in town."

"You're nothing but a fucking bitch. I should have killed you earlier, not just beat the crap out of you."

"I figured your brother was the one pulling all these stunts, and you were just yanking his chain, as always."

He glared at her. "My brother didn't do nothing. I was

yanking *your* chain."

"You mean, nothing bad, *yet*," she added. "So are you the one who sent all those bullets flying into my house? Snuck into my house, left the bullet on my railing…"

He shrugged. "Those were just scare tactics. Like I said, messing with your head. I mean everyone already believes you're a nut, this just adds to it. Besides that's nothing."

"Right, so coming into my house and holding a detective hostage is what? A logical next step?"

"For me, yeah. Too bad this guy got involved, especially when he's probably close to retirement age," he said, with a smirk. "But, if you think I'll let you ruin my career in the military, you've got another think coming."

"The military was always your playground," she stated. "It's like they gave you some sort of permission to be an absolute asshole."

"They did," he agreed. "I get to do this to all kinds of women. It was better though when I was out in the field because those women, the foreign ones?" He waggled his eyebrows. "They never had any chance to argue."

She stiffened at that. "So why did you fixate on me?"

"Because you fucking turned me down," he snapped. "I had always wondered what it would be like to take you to bed. Now, of course, that's just disgusting." He looked down at her missing leg, and he shuddered. "You know what? I should just put you down and put you out of your misery." Then he realized that Rhys also was missing a leg. And Colby started to laugh. "You're both just a matched pair of cripples. God, and here I thought maybe this guy would be some competition, but he's not. You're both just losers." He shook his head and nudged the detective. "Even this guy won't give me much of a run for my money."

"What do you care about a run for your money?" she asked, trying to figure out how to get the hell out of this situation. "I mean, you only pick on people who are injured or damaged in some way or vulnerable. The women off in those countries where you were sent for missions, did the military never figure it out?"

"Nope. And anybody who wanted to say anything, I usually just intimidated them, or they had an accident." He sneered. "The military is my playground. It gives me a license to do what I love to do anyway. And now that I get a chance to do it, I'm getting better and better at it too."

She stared at him, realizing that he had basically admitted to being a serial killer in training. "And have you killed anybody whom you raped?" she whispered.

He nodded, with a fat smile. "Yeah, a couple. And I really like how it feels. I love that sense of power."

"It's not power." She glared at him. "It's a weakness. It's a sickness. And you're the sick puppy who thinks it's okay."

"It is okay, and nobody'll stop me. So why the hell do I need you around to make my life miserable?"

"You're just afraid that whatever I do will stop you," she said, smiling at him. "I mean, I'm the one who survived."

"You didn't survive nothing." He glared at her. "I didn't do nothing to you."

"If you didn't, who did then?" she asked, gazing at him, willing him to talk and to give her some of the answers that she needed.

"You were just a lesson to somebody, but then I realized that I liked the feel of your fear," he explained. "I wanted to torment you a little bit more, a little bit longer, before I had sex with you."

"*Had sex with me?* As if I don't have any say in the matter?"

"You don't," he stated. "I'll take whoever the hell I want. And, if it happens to be you, you should be damn happy that I gave you five minutes of my time."

"That must mean that you only last five minutes in bed," she noted bluntly.

At that, he bolted to his feet and glared at her. "Oh no you don't. I'm not so easy to get sidelined."

"Are you sure?" she asked. "Because obviously the detective sidelined you. You're holding a gun to his head, and it looks like you've already hit him over the head a few times too," she said, studying the poor man.

He had a black eye, and his nose was starting to swell, but still a glint remained in his gaze.

"What the hell did you do to my dog?"

"The fucking dog, at least it has four legs. Maybe I'll take him with me. I mean, if he's really a War Dog, he should have some killing abilities too."

"What? So now you'll send the dog to do your dirty work?"

"Why not? That'd probably be pretty fun to watch." He shook his head. "Regardless I am done with you guys. Like how the hell is any of this even an issue? You should have just disappeared from sight, and I wouldn't even be in this position."

"And, if you hadn't attacked me multiple times," she noted, "I wouldn't have been in this position to do something about it."

"And you didn't have to do anything about it," he snapped. "Just take it. You're nothing but a female anyway."

She stared at him, wondering if he'd always had that attitude. "And what about Andrew?"

"What about him? Apparently he's quite pissed at my brother." He shrugged. "I don't give a shit. He'll get over it. It's not like he's a friend worth keeping anymore."

"Why? Because he doesn't understand what you do?"

"No, he sure doesn't. I did try to tell him once or twice, but he was pretty pissed about the whole thing."

"Gee, what a surprise. Somebody who doesn't agree with you."

"I mean, I may have to take him out somewhere down the road—especially after I had that talk with him to see whether he would be on my side or not, to see if maybe he'd get involved in some local games here," he said, with a shrug. "But he didn't seem to like the idea too much."

"Well, I don't think he's very good friends with me either. He seemed pretty pissed that I'd even talk to him."

"Yeah, I told him about you, but I gave him *my* side of the story," he said, with a ghostly smile. "It's not as if he'll believe you."

"No, of course not." She had already mentally crossed Andrew off her list. "Still, you can't always win."

"Sure as hell I can," he snapped. "I've been getting better and better at this over the last couple years. I'm just to the point now where I'm really good at it and where most people won't ever find out. But you're still part of my history, something that needs to be taken care of, and after this? Well, I mean, the world's my oyster. I get sent all over the world. And those third-world countries, those women, they don't know what hit them."

"Wow," she said, "so once again you terrorize people who have absolutely no way to fight you off. So how fair is that?"

"I don't give a shit if it's fair or not," he replied in a

bored tone. He looked over at Rhys. "God, he's not … I mean, Jesus, just looking at your legs like that. That's just wrong," he stated, with an outward shudder.

She stared at him. "No wonder you're such a child still. What kind of attitude is that?"

"Oh, stop lecturing me," Colby said. "You were such a bore, all those years ago growing up. You always thought people should be nice. Instead I just wanted to torment you some more every time you were nice. It just spurred me on to be meaner. Don't you get it? Only the bad guys win."

"Says you," she spat, with spirit, glaring at him. "You never used to be this much of an asshole."

"That's all you know about," he said, with a grin. "I got plenty of asshole in my history. You just don't know about it."

She stared at him and winced. "And I probably don't."

"Nope, you sure don't. Anyway, I don't have time for this," he said. "I've gotta get back to the base and catch my ride back to Germany."

"Oh, I don't think you'll be going anywhere," she noted.

"Oh, yeah I am," he said, with a smile. "Ain't nothing you and your crippled partner over there can do to me to stop me. And, this old cop here, he's got nothing left in him."

"Why did you have to beat him up?" she asked in fury. "That's hardly decent."

"I also beat up the dog." He grinned at her evilly. "I needed to take out my temper on something. He thought I was a friend, but believe me. He knows better now."

Her heart sank because she realized that Tallahassee was hurt too. She took several steps with her crutches toward the living room.

"Oh no you don't," Colby said. "No way in hell you're going anywhere."

"Yes, I will," she snapped. "I'll go see what you did to my dog." He laughed at that, but she had moved just enough to the side that she could see Tallahassee. He was coming out of whatever stupor he'd been, as he slowly got up on his legs.

She winced. "God, did you have to hurt him? Tallahassee, stay there. Don't try to move."

"Oh, is he alive?" Colby asked, as he hopped to his feet, took a step, keeping the gun trained on the detective. "I'll have to pop him now. He'll look as bad as you guys. That's just a mercy killing now. Times three," he said, with raucous laughter.

And he cocked the gun. Just as he went to fire it, she grabbed his arm, and the gun went off harmlessly. He reached around, smacked her hard, and sent her flying to the ground, but already both the detective and Rhys jumped Colby. And both of them might have been already injured and or struggling with something physically, but they were certainly strong enough to overpower Colby. Just as they went to take away the gun, Colby managed to get back to his feet and raced into the living room.

And right into Tallahassee, who sunk his teeth into Colby's shoulder and took him down.

RHYS STEPPED FORWARD in front of Tallahassee. "Easy, boy, take it easy."

At that, the dog growled at Colby, and his hackles went up even higher.

"I know. He beat you up, and he deserves whatever he's

got coming," Rhys said, "and not just you but other people want Colby to suffer too. But this isn't the way."

The dog just glared at Rhys, never releasing his hold on Colby.

Rhys gave Tallahassee a set of sharp commands, and, after a moment's hesitation, finally Tallahassee dropped the shoulder of what appeared to be an unconscious man. At that, Rhys called Tallahassee to heel, and Tallahassee, moving slowly, came toward Rhys and sat down at his side. He bent down to him, while the detective ran and Taylor crutched over to the downed man.

The detective quickly cuffed Colby, while she checked for a pulse. "He's alive." She stared over at the detective and winced. "I'm so sorry."

He gave her a hard look. "It's not your fault, but no way in hell is this guy getting loose now."

She got up, crutched over to bend down in front of Tallahassee, her hand gently going out to the injured dog. "We're taking you to a vet right now," she told Tallahassee. She looked back at the detective. "Can you stay here with Colby and wait for your team?"

He nodded immediately. "Get the dog some help," he said. "He deserves it."

And, with that, Rhys helped Tallahassee out the door, while Taylor slowly headed toward the passenger's side on her crutches and opened the door. Tallahassee couldn't jump up. Rhys placed the dog carefully in the passenger seat. He looked over at her.

She nodded. "I'll sit in the back." She quickly bailed into the back seat, and they drove to the vet. She crutched it inside letting them know she had an emergency.

The vet looked at her and asked, "The War Dog?"

She nodded. "Yes."

"We got a call from a detective."

She nodded and pointed. "That's him."

And, with a gurney, they came outside, and Rhys came around and lifted up the dog, who was whining in pain in the back of his throat. He carefully placed the dog on the gurney, looked over at the vet, and said, "Whatever it takes."

The vet's eyebrows shot up, but he nodded. "Let's hope he's salvageable." And, with that, he disappeared inside.

With Rhys at her side, she crutched it inside and sat down in the waiting room. When the receptionist called out, Rhys got the new account form and gave it to Taylor to fill out, and then sat back down beside her.

"You know, this visit could be expensive," she said.

"Doesn't matter," Rhys stated.

"Could be thousands and thousands."

"Doesn't matter," he repeated.

She smiled and slipped her hand down to link her fingers with his. "See? That's what I like in a man," she said. "Somebody who understands priorities."

He squeezed her fingers gently, and they waited in almost silence, while he texted to his bosses and gave them an update.

"At least it's over now," she said.

He nodded. "As soon as I get confirmation that the asshole's been locked up, it is."

"You don't think he'll come after us again, will he?"

"Only if he escapes custody."

At that, her gaze went huge, and she sank back in horror. "Hopefully not."

When his phone went off a few minutes later, he answered it. "Hey. Did you get him in custody?" And with that answer, he sagged in relief, looked at her, and gave her a thumbs-up. He continued to listen to the detective, giving Rhys a further rundown.

"Good enough," he said, "thanks for the update." He hung up, looked over at her, and smiled. "He's in jail. The medic came and took a look at him, and he'll need some stitches. So they're arranging security at the hospital right now, so he can get taken care of."

"Right. That won't rebound on Tallahassee, will it?" she asked, biting on her lower lip.

"No, I don't think so. The dog was badly beaten first, and Colby came at him again, so the dog had full rights to understand that it would be another beating. So self-defense should count in that case. And then we have the added facts that Colby had already injured you several times, and beat up a cop, so I don't think anybody'll be feeling too particular about the ins and outs of whether the dog did something illegal or not. Plus Django reported these incidents to Colby's commanding officer, so the army is aware of all this too."

She shook her head. "I can't believe that Colby got into the house, and we didn't even know."

"We also don't know how long he was in the house for."

She winced at that. "Presumably not very long but why didn't we hear Tallahassee barking at an intruder?"

"And that's something that'll take a bit to figure out," he stated. "Who knows? Colby may have drugged the dog, just like he did with you. Regardless we will work on Tallahassee's training again. He's had quite a few months where everything kind of slipped on him."

"And yet it's not Tallahassee's fault," she stated instantly.

"No, it isn't," he agreed, "and I can certainly help him to

get back on track again."

"I think he got his priorities just fine," she said. "I know I don't want to let him go."

"And no need to either," he replied, with a gentle smile.

She glanced nervously over at the door, where the vet had gone with Tallahassee, and said, "It's taking a long time."

Rhys nodded and squeezed her fingers gently. In another fifteen, twenty minutes she got up and started pacing. Then realized that the crutches made her sore under her arms, so she sat back down again. And just then the internal door opened, and the vet stepped out.

He looked at them, a half smile on his face, and said, "The dog will live. He's got a cracked femur, a couple bruised ribs, one cracked rib," he explained, "plus the hip was dislocated, and there appears to be quite substantial bruising. Whoever worked him over did a good job."

"Yeah, well, that asshole's in jail right now," she snapped. She grabbed her crutches and stood. "You can fix him?"

He nodded. "Everything's fixable," he confirmed gently.

She sagged back down again, relief on her face, then looked over at Rhys and smiled, teary-eyed. "He'll be okay."

"Just not for a day or two," the vet clarified.

She looked at him in surprise. "Meaning?"

"Meaning, he can't go home with you yet. I want to straighten that leg, and I've already put the hip back in place," he added. "Definitely a few adjustments can be made. I just want to keep him overnight."

"Fine, but only overnight," she said, frowning at him.

He gave her a glimmer of a smile. "Got it." He looked at Rhys. "Is he still dangerous?"

Rhys immediately shook his head. "He was badly beaten

by this guy. So when Tallahassee attacked Colby, it was to defend himself, thinking a second beating was coming. This same guy had also just beaten the crap out of a local police detective too."

At that, the vet's eyes widened. "Crap. Well, Tallahassee definitely needs to be rescued, so leave him with us overnight. I'll keep him drugged up pretty well, and I can get those few adjustments done, and we'll go from there. With any luck, he can come home with you in the morning."

And, with that, Rhys and Taylor got up, and he stepped outside wrapping his arm around her shoulders.

She took a slow deep breath and whispered, "I'm so happy he'll make it."

He looked down at her, his lips twitching. "I guess that means you're keeping him."

"Nope," she said, "*we're* keeping him."

He stared at her, and then a slow smile dawned. "Ah, back to that long-term thing?"

She nodded, and he held her gently, helping her keep her balance on her crutches. "Absolutely, unless you've got a problem with that?"

"No," he said, "no arguments from me." He looked over at the truck and lifted his chin. "Come on. Let's go home."

And he thought to himself, no better word than *home* in the dictionary. It seemed like, for a very long time, he hadn't known what *home* was and hadn't had one to even call *home*, but now that had all changed. He looked down at her and added, "Unless you've got a problem with that."

She shook her head. "I don't think I ever knew what a home was before now," she whispered.

"In that case, let's go find out together."

And, with his arm lightly on her shoulder, they slowly moved toward the truck and then to her place.

EPILOGUE

KAT BROUGHT A cup of coffee for Badger and placed it in front of him, then she sat down herself. "So another good ending," she said, with satisfaction.

"I think more than either of us expected in this case," Badger murmured.

"At this point in time"—she chuckled—"I'm expecting the best on every case."

"Maybe, … it was definitely not a sure thing there."

"And do we have any update on Taylor's military assault case?"

"Yes, the army is doing a full investigation and looking into why she wasn't dealt with fairly in the first place." Badger smiled. "That should shake things up pretty well."

"It needs to happen," Kat stated.

Badger nodded. "It's a sad world where men are allowed to prey on women, no matter what the industry," he noted. He picked up a file sitting in front of him and dropped it in front of her. "Since you were so helpful on the last one …"

"You mean, on the last couple," she stated, flashing him a big grin.

He added, "I'm only letting you get away with that because I love you."

"I know you are." Chuckling, she opened up the file and asked, "And who is this War Dog?"

"Her name's Chica."

Kat studied the picture of the beautiful shepherd Malinois–looking cross. "And what's her story?"

"She was sent down to Mexico and somehow ended up in one of those large shipments, where the dogs go from Mexico up to Canada."

She raised her gaze to him and frowned. "What? How did Chica end up in Mexico?"

"We don't know that, but it looks like our War Dog was adopted by a man out of Texas, who became an ex-pat when he moved to Mexico, where he took the dog with him."

"And then …?" Kat waited.

"We don't know. He's deceased now, and the dog was shipped to Canada. And we're not sure where Chica is."

"They tend to keep really good records on transports like that."

"Sure," he agreed, "but, when the shipment got there, apparently Chica didn't arrive in Canada."

"Well, crap. Did the shipment touch down anywhere in-between?"

"Some came by plane. Some came by train. Ones with health conditions were transported via a combo of trucking, then flying. A planeload was sent over our northern border with about seventy-five dogs on that flight."

"And Chica wasn't on the plane."

He shook his head. "No."

"So she's got health conditions."

"That's what our assumption is."

"And what about the rest of them in that truckload?"

"Everyone arrived except for three."

She winced. "And of course Chica is one of the three."

He nodded. "The truck driver says that the cages went

missing from the truck on the last leg. No idea how that happened. The other problem is that Chica is not completely whole. She's missing half a paw, and she's had a leg broken in multiple places."

"Which is why, of course, she ended up in the not-so-healthy group."

"That's partly it, but there could be a lot of other things wrong with her now."

"So where did they cross the border?"

"New York."

She stared at him. "That's not exactly a city for a dog."

"Nope, doesn't mean that the dog is even in New York."

"No, of course not. ... Niagara Falls, I presume?"

He laughed. "And how did you guess?"

"The biggest border crossing," she said, with a sigh.

"There's a lot of paperwork that has to be done, and there was a problem at the border. Some of the paperwork wasn't quite up to snuff. So they pulled the truck and the dogs off to the side, and apparently they went missing then—somewhere in that time frame, while the handler was taking down the cages, opening them up, letting the dogs out, taking them for walks, putting them back in again."

"And yet he says three of the cages went missing."

Badger nodded. "He didn't know what to do, so he headed on to the next destination with the rest of the dogs and reported it."

Kat sighed. "And Chica could be anywhere."

"That's the problem right now—that's Chica's issue. We still have to find somebody who can go track down Chica. That's *our* issue."

She looked over at her husband. "You got anybody in mind?"

"Nope, I sure don't. I've pretty well tapped out everybody we've got locally. You?"

She thought about it and frowned. "I do have one guy I've been dealing with back and forth. He's from that area."

"Well, maybe contact him?"

She frowned, pulled out her phone, flicked through her contacts, and when she finally got to the one in question, she said, "I just don't know what he's up for."

"Why is he contacting you?"

"He lost one leg and one hand," she stated.

"How?"

"Bomb squad."

"Military?"

She nodded. "Yes. So chances are he's had some workings with the military animals."

"Are we even sure that he has? It depends more so on whether he has a soft heart and whether he has any compassion and whether he has any ability to get around right now."

She quickly phoned him, and, when she got him at the other end, there was surprise in his voice.

"Hey, Kat. What's up?"

She quickly explained the problem.

He sighed. "I'm due to have surgery."

"Oh, crap, I forgot. Well, hey, that's, ... that's okay. We'll keep looking."

"Hey, ... I've got an idea," he said, "but that depends on whether my brother would be okay with it."

"And what's your brother doing right now?"

"Well, he was looking after a buddy of his, who just passed away. They were both in the same unit in Iran, and they both got shot up pretty badly. When his buddy started to go downhill, my brother basically stopped his move forward in life to help him out. But now his buddy is gone."

"Oh, good Lord," she said. "That's gotta be hard."

"Pretty devastating for him, yes. And he does have his buddy's dogs now, so I'm not sure whether he'd be free or not."

"What kind of dogs?"

He laughed at that. "You'd think that, you know, somebody like my brother would have Shepherds or Newfoundlands or something huge," he explained. "Instead he's got these tiny, tiny-ass Chihuahuas."

She snickered.

He said, "Right? Anyway let me contact him, and, if he's interested, I'll get him to call you."

"Sounds good." She disconnected the call, looked over at Badger, and shrugged. "All we can do is try."

He agreed. "And we'll keep looking at our end."

At that, they sipped their coffee and went through a bunch of other paperwork they had to deal with.

When her phone rang, she looked at it and said, "I don't know the number." She answered it and found it was the brother on the other end.

"My name is Landon," he stated. "My brother just contacted me, told me about how you're looking for a missing War Dog."

"Yes." She hesitated, then continued. "We just need a little bit more clarity about if you have any experience and if something like this would even be of interest to you."

"Well, I'm at loose ends," he shared, his voice roughening slightly. "I could use a distraction."

"Good enough," she replied. "Do you have anybody to keep you from fulfilling this job?"

"No, but I presume I won't die on the job."

"No, I wouldn't think so," she stated, "but I would be remiss in not telling you that some of the previous War Dog scenarios have been pretty rough."

"Yeah, well, that's life right now," he said. "So tell me more about it."

By the time she put the call on Speakerphone, and she and Badger explained everything, Landon replied, "You know what? I think I heard about these dogs, and the job you're doing. A friend of mine, Blaze, told me."

"Do you know Blaze?" Badger asked.

"Yeah," Landon confirmed. "I worked with him overseas a couple times."

"Yes, Blaze is definitely somebody who has helped us out."

"Well, in that case," Landon said, "I guess I can do my part for the War Dog too." He hesitated and then asked, "When would you need me?"

"As soon as possible," Badger said. "The dog's been lost for a while, and now we have to find out what's happening with it."

"And what if I can't find her?"

"Then it's a case of *you tried*," Badger noted simply. "So far we haven't *not* located any of our assigned War Dogs, but it could happen. We keep expecting it to happen, but, so far, we've been blessed to find them."

"Well, that puts the pressure on," Landon said, with a wry note.

"And yet we're not doing it for that reason," she jumped in to say.

"No, I got it," Landon confirmed.

Kat leaned forward. "Your brother said you were injured."

"Yeah, I am. Lost a foot just about three inches above the ankle. I've got a prosthetic." Then he stopped and asked, "Does that change anything?"

"No, not in my world."

"Or mine," Badger agreed. "Kat, my wife here, is working with your brother on his prosthetics."

"Oh my," he said, "*that* Kat." He laughed. "Hey, do I get a prosthetic out of this deal?"

"Do you need one?" she asked curiously.

"The one I've got sucks," he stated.

"You have no idea how often I hear that," she murmured. "I'll tell you what. I can't promise anything, but, if we can get this job done, I'll take a good look at it."

"Hey, that'd be perfect," he said, "and I gather there's no money involved in finding the War Dogs."

"No."

"Good. Jobs like this shouldn't require a paycheck to get them done—although I won't be adverse to getting some expenses reimbursed."

"That we can do," Badger declared. "I'll email all this information to you. Let me know what your itinerary is, as soon as you sort it out. And check-ins, please, on a regular basis."

"You got it," Landon said and hung up.

Badger looked over at Kat and grinned. "Not bad," he said. "Not exactly the way we thought it would work, but, hey, we'll take it." And he held up a hand to high-five her.

She smiled and added, "Now if only we get another happy relationship outta this one too."

He rolled his eyes. "Let's get a happy dog first," he said, "and a relationship's secondary."

"It is, until it isn't," she declared, with a smile. "All these guys deserve to be happy, and it sounds like this guy needs it even more than most."

Badger raised an eyebrow at that.

She shrugged. "Not many guys would take time out of their lives to help their buddy on the last of his days."

Badger nodded slowly at that. "You got that right. Guys like that are few and far between."

With that, she closed the file and slid it back to him. "Let's hope he finds somebody who recognizes just how special he is."

This concludes Book 17 of The K9 Files: Rhys.
Read about Landon: The K9 Files, Book 18

THE K9 FILES: LANDON (BOOK #18)

Welcome to the all new K9 Files series reconnecting readers with the unforgettable men from SEALs of Steel in a new series of action packed, page turning romantic suspense that fans have come to expect from USA TODAY Bestselling author Dale Mayer. Pssst... you'll meet other favorite characters from SEALs of Honor and Heroes for Hire too!

Landon, after a tough couple of years helping his navy buddy live out his last years, needed a break. Tracking a war dog named Chico to make sure it was okay sounded perfect. Especially being able to take his three chihuahuas with him. But finding a dog that had been part of a large shipment heading to a rescue across the Canadian border but had gone missing on the last stop before the border – well that was going to be a challenge. Particularly one that had a lame leg and half a paw.

Sabrina had spent years volunteering at a local vet clinic, because all animals had a soft spot in her heart. Finding Landon is trying to track down a missing War Dog, well how could she not volunteer to help him? Still when her world flips upside down, she's more than happy to have Landon close by.

Now if only they could find the dog and figure out who and what was responsible for endangering her life...

Find Book 18 here!

To find out more visit Dale Mayer's website.

http://smarturl.it/DMLandonUniversal

Author's Note

Thank you for reading Rhys: The K9 Files, Book 17! If you enjoyed the book, please take a moment and leave a short review.

Dear reader,

I love to hear from readers, and you can contact me at my website: www.dalemayer.com or at my Facebook author page. To be informed of new releases and special offers, sign up for my newsletter or follow me on BookBub. And if you are interested in joining Dale Mayer's Reader Group, here is the Facebook sign up page. https://smarturl.it/DaleMayerFBGroup

Cheers,
Dale Mayer

Get THREE Free Books Now!

Have you met the SEALS of Honor?

SEALs of Honor Books 1, 2, and 3. Follow the stories of brave, badass warriors who serve their country with honor and love their women to the limits of life and death.

Read Mason, Hawk, and Dane right now for FREE.

Go here and tell me where to send them!
http://smarturl.it/EthanBofB

About the Author

Dale Mayer is a *USA Today* best-selling author, best known for her SEALs military romances, her Psychic Visions series, and her Lovely Lethal Garden cozy series. Her contemporary romances are raw and full of passion and emotion (Broken But ... Mending, Hathaway House series). Her thrillers will keep you guessing (Kate Morgan, By Death series), and her romantic comedies will keep you giggling (*It's a Dog's Life*, a stand-alone novella; and the Broken Protocols series, starring Charming Marvin, the cat).

Dale honors the stories that come to her—and some of them are crazy, break all the rules and cross multiple genres!

To go with her fiction, she also writes nonfiction in many different fields, with books available on résumé writing, companion gardening, and the US mortgage system. All her books are available in print and ebook format.

Connect with Dale Mayer Online

Dale's Website – www.dalemayer.com

Twitter – @DaleMayer

Facebook Page – geni.us/DaleMayerFBFanPage

Facebook Group – geni.us/DaleMayerFBGroup

BookBub – geni.us/DaleMayerBookbub

Instagram – geni.us/DaleMayerInstagram

Goodreads – geni.us/DaleMayerGoodreads

Newsletter – geni.us/DaleNews

Also by Dale Mayer

Published Adult Books:

Shadow Recon
Magnus, Book 1

Bullard's Battle
Ryland's Reach, Book 1
Cain's Cross, Book 2
Eton's Escape, Book 3
Garret's Gambit, Book 4
Kano's Keep, Book 5
Fallon's Flaw, Book 6
Quinn's Quest, Book 7
Bullard's Beauty, Book 8
Bullard's Best, Book 9
Bullard's Battle, Books 1–2
Bullard's Battle, Books 3–4
Bullard's Battle, Books 5–6
Bullard's Battle, Books 7–8

Terkel's Team
Damon's Deal, Book 1
Wade's War, Book 2
Gage's Goal, Book 3
Calum's Contact, Book 4
Rick's Road, Book 5

Scott's Summit, Book 6
Brody's Beast, Book 7

Kate Morgan
Simon Says... Hide, Book 1
Simon Says... Jump, Book 2
Simon Says... Ride, Book 3
Simon Says... Scream, Book 4
Simon Says... Run, Book 5

Hathaway House
Aaron, Book 1
Brock, Book 2
Cole, Book 3
Denton, Book 4
Elliot, Book 5
Finn, Book 6
Gregory, Book 7
Heath, Book 8
Iain, Book 9
Jaden, Book 10
Keith, Book 11
Lance, Book 12
Melissa, Book 13
Nash, Book 14
Owen, Book 15
Percy, Book 16
Quinton, Book 17
Ryatt, Book 18
Hathaway House, Books 1–3
Hathaway House, Books 4–6
Hathaway House, Books 7–9

The K9 Files

Lovely Lethal Gardens

Psychic Vision Series

Eye of the Falcon
Itsy-Bitsy Spider
Unmasked
Deep Beneath
From the Ashes
Stroke of Death
Ice Maiden
Snap, Crackle…
What If…
Talking Bones
String of Tears
Psychic Visions Books 1–3
Psychic Visions Books 4–6
Psychic Visions Books 7–9

By Death Series
Touched by Death
Haunted by Death
Chilled by Death
By Death Books 1–3

Broken Protocols – Romantic Comedy Series
Cat's Meow
Cat's Pajamas
Cat's Cradle
Cat's Claus
Broken Protocols 1-4

Broken and… Mending
Skin
Scars
Scales (of Justice)
Broken but… Mending 1-3

Glory

Genesis

Tori

Celeste

Glory Trilogy

Biker Blues

Morgan: Biker Blues, Volume 1

Cash: Biker Blues, Volume 2

SEALs of Honor

Mason: SEALs of Honor, Book 1

Hawk: SEALs of Honor, Book 2

Dane: SEALs of Honor, Book 3

Swede: SEALs of Honor, Book 4

Shadow: SEALs of Honor, Book 5

Cooper: SEALs of Honor, Book 6

Markus: SEALs of Honor, Book 7

Evan: SEALs of Honor, Book 8

Mason's Wish: SEALs of Honor, Book 9

Chase: SEALs of Honor, Book 10

Brett: SEALs of Honor, Book 11

Devlin: SEALs of Honor, Book 12

Easton: SEALs of Honor, Book 13

Ryder: SEALs of Honor, Book 14

Macklin: SEALs of Honor, Book 15

Corey: SEALs of Honor, Book 16

Warrick: SEALs of Honor, Book 17

Tanner: SEALs of Honor, Book 18

Jackson: SEALs of Honor, Book 19

Kanen: SEALs of Honor, Book 20

Nelson: SEALs of Honor, Book 21

Taylor: SEALs of Honor, Book 22

Colton: SEALs of Honor, Book 23
Troy: SEALs of Honor, Book 24
Axel: SEALs of Honor, Book 25
Baylor: SEALs of Honor, Book 26
Hudson: SEALs of Honor, Book 27
Lachlan: SEALs of Honor, Book 28
Paxton: SEALs of Honor, Book 29
SEALs of Honor, Books 1–3
SEALs of Honor, Books 4–6
SEALs of Honor, Books 7–10
SEALs of Honor, Books 11–13
SEALs of Honor, Books 14–16
SEALs of Honor, Books 17–19
SEALs of Honor, Books 20–22
SEALs of Honor, Books 23–25

Heroes for Hire
Levi's Legend: Heroes for Hire, Book 1
Stone's Surrender: Heroes for Hire, Book 2
Merk's Mistake: Heroes for Hire, Book 3
Rhodes's Reward: Heroes for Hire, Book 4
Flynn's Firecracker: Heroes for Hire, Book 5
Logan's Light: Heroes for Hire, Book 6
Harrison's Heart: Heroes for Hire, Book 7
Saul's Sweetheart: Heroes for Hire, Book 8
Dakota's Delight: Heroes for Hire, Book 9
Tyson's Treasure: Heroes for Hire, Book 10
Jace's Jewel: Heroes for Hire, Book 11
Rory's Rose: Heroes for Hire, Book 12
Brandon's Bliss: Heroes for Hire, Book 13
Liam's Lily: Heroes for Hire, Book 14
North's Nikki: Heroes for Hire, Book 15

SEALs of Steel

SEALs of Steel, Books 5–8
SEALs of Steel, Books 1–8

The Mavericks

Kerrick, Book 1
Griffin, Book 2
Jax, Book 3
Beau, Book 4
Asher, Book 5
Ryker, Book 6
Miles, Book 7
Nico, Book 8
Keane, Book 9
Lennox, Book 10
Gavin, Book 11
Shane, Book 12
Diesel, Book 13
Jerricho, Book 14
Killian, Book 15
Hatch, Book 16
Corbin, Book 17
Aiden, Book 18
The Mavericks, Books 1–2
The Mavericks, Books 3–4
The Mavericks, Books 5–6
The Mavericks, Books 7–8
The Mavericks, Books 9–10
The Mavericks, Books 11–12

Collections

Dare to Be You…
Dare to Love…
Dare to be Strong…

RomanceX3

Standalone Novellas
It's a Dog's Life
Riana's Revenge
Second Chances

Published Young Adult Books:

Family Blood Ties Series
Vampire in Denial
Vampire in Distress
Vampire in Design
Vampire in Deceit
Vampire in Defiance
Vampire in Conflict
Vampire in Chaos
Vampire in Crisis
Vampire in Control
Vampire in Charge
Family Blood Ties Set 1–3
Family Blood Ties Set 1–5
Family Blood Ties Set 4–6
Family Blood Ties Set 7–9
Sian's Solution, A Family Blood Ties Series Prequel
    Novelette

Design series
Dangerous Designs
Deadly Designs
Darkest Designs
Design Series Trilogy

Standalone

In Cassie's Corner
Gem Stone (a Gemma Stone Mystery)
Time Thieves

Published Non-Fiction Books:

Career Essentials

Career Essentials: The Résumé
Career Essentials: The Cover Letter
Career Essentials: The Interview
Career Essentials: 3 in 1

Made in United States
North Haven, CT
13 September 2022

24052060R00134